THE BONNIE BLUE

JOAN ELLIOTT PICKART

D1441324

BANTAM BOOKS
NEW YORK • TORONTO • LONDON • SYDNEY • AUCKLAND

This edition contains the complete text
of the original hardcover edition.
Not one word has been omitted.

THE BONNIE BLUE

A Bantam Fanfare Book / July 1991

PRINTING HISTORY

Doubleday edition published August 1990

ISBN 0-553-29090-8

Published simultaneously in the United States and Canada

Bantam Books are published by Bantam Books, a division of Bantam
Doubleday Dell Publishing Group, Inc. Its trademark, consisting of the words
"Bantam Books" and the portrayal of a rooster, is Registered in U.S. Patent
and Trademark Office and in other countries. Marca Registrada. Bantam
Books, 666 Fifth Avenue, New York, New York 10103.

PRINTED IN THE UNITED STATES OF AMERICA

OPM   0   9   8   7   6   5   4   3   2   1

With special thanks to Elizabeth Barrett,
who went the extra mile

THE BONNIE BLUE

One

The saloon was crowded and noisy. It was Saturday night, payday, and the cowboys were out in force. The randy men had a number of pleasure palaces to choose from in Dodge City, Kansas, but the Silver Spur was by far the most popular. The Spur had the prettiest women—all ready, willing, and able—and the best piano player. The whiskey wasn't watered down and the card dealers were honest.

And the Silver Spur was fancy. A man felt important just walking through the swinging doors. Crystal chandeliers hung from the ceiling, their multitude of candles lighting the large main room as bright as day. The bar was a gleaming slab of highly polished mahogany, the mirror behind it reflecting the room into infinity. The women wore fancy dresses of velvet or taffeta with matching feathers in their hair. All of the Spur's fine trimmings had been brought in from the East, and the men of Dodge enjoyed the elegance, so different from the long hours they spent in the saddle, breathing in dust and the stink of cattle.

The Silver Spur was special, and it belonged to Mattie Muldoon.

Mattie stood at the top of the stairs and scrutinized the activity below. With a practiced and knowing eye, she could pick out the young cowboy who was close to having too much to drink; could pinpoint the strangers, and in one quick glance know who was potential trouble and who was there just for a good time.

But this Saturday night, she scanned the boisterous crowd looking for one man. He had to be there. She needed him to be there. Her heart beat wildly as she searched the room, hoping, hoping . . . Yes!

He was playing cards, his chair tilted back to lean against the wall. His Stetson was pushed up to reveal thick, black hair and sharp, handsome profile. His skin was bronzed by heritage and sun, his eyes as dark as the devil's. A gray western shirt stretched across his broad shoulders and chest, and Mattie knew well the rest of his rugged body. He was tall, more than six feet, with taut, hard muscles. Big and dark, magnificent and dangerous, he was a man all women fantasized about.

His name was Slade Ironbow.

Half Apache Indian, Slade had, in Mattie's opinion, the best attributes of his Indian father and white mother. He moved with the smooth, controlled grace of the Indian, and had a sixth sense that helped him survive a rough and wild country.

He stepped into the white man's world when he chose, and no one said more than once that he didn't belong there. A mere look from Slade's cold, obsidian eyes could pin a man in place. Those who pushed too far, who recklessly challenged him, felt the bullet from the gun that left Slade's holster with the speed of quicksilver.

Slade answered to no one, and Mattie never knew when

he might appear in Dodge. She suspected that he disappeared into the hills to spend time with his father's people, but he never told her. She never asked. Wild, contradictory rumors forever circulated about Slade, but she gave none of them credence. She'd believe only what he told her.

He'd returned to Dodge three days earlier, after being gone for two months. She'd greeted him without question, as though he'd never left. It had been like that for many years, and Mattie didn't expect it ever to change.

Slade Ironbow was thirty-two years old to Mattie's thirty-eight, and she loved him like a brother. Everyone believed they were lovers, when in actuality Slade was her best friend. And tonight she needed him more than she ever had before.

She slowly descended the stairs, nodding and smiling at those who greeted her. She forced herself not to rush to Slade's side and beg him to come upstairs, where they could be alone and she could pour out her heart to him.

Catching a glimpse of herself in the sparkling mirror over the bar, she studied her reflection, wondering if anyone could tell she was deeply distressed.

Her dark red hair was piled high on her head, with a few unruly tendrils curling along her slender neck. The emerald green of her silk dress was the exact shade of her eyes.

Her full breasts pushed above the low-cut, lace-edged bodice, enticing a second look from appreciative male eyes. The fact that it now took whalebone stays to give her breasts the lift they needed was nobody's business but her own. No one saw her naked body, for she was the owner of the Silver Spur now, and since Slade had come into her life, she no longer made her living by taking unwanted men into her bed.

Whenever any stranger pestered her, trying to buy her for an hour, or for the night, her bartender quickly and quietly informed him that she was Slade Ironbow's woman. The poor man would mumble his apologies and back away, disappearing into the crowd. No one, however, questioned Slade's enjoying the services of her girls. That was simply accepted as characteristic of an extremely virile man whom one woman would never satisfy. The charade with Slade served her well, and she was continually grateful for his compliance.

Mattie glanced at him again, wondering how long he and the three other men would play poker. Two of the men were wealthy ranchers; Mattie had seen them and Slade play through until dawn. Not tonight, she pleaded silently. Please, not tonight.

The other man was Doc Willis, who had been tending to the illnesses and injuries of the citizens of Dodge since before Mattie had come there more than twenty years ago. On any other night, she would have indulged in a moment's daydreaming about Doc Willis. She had loved him for years, and had kept that love a secret. She could never tell him.

With one last look at Slade, she turned away. The anxiety within her churned fiercely, and she could taste the metallic flavor of fear. Still, as she circulated through the growing crowd for the next hour, she managed to maintain her image of elegance, combined with an air of touch-me-not. Many a young cowboy followed her unhurried movements with his gaze, his heart and fantasies racing.

Mattie knew it the instant the two ranchers with Slade stood up, laughing and shaking their heads in defeat. A sob of relief nearly escaped her lips as the men ambled away, eyeing the girls who were still available. She walked toward Slade, instructing herself to move slowly, to smile.

"Well," she said, laying one hand on Slade's shoulder, "you scared those two off early tonight. Cleaned them out, by the looks of it. You and Doc seem to have won about the same amount."

"We did all right," Slade said.

His voice was dark and deep. One of Mattie's girls had said that Slade could undress a woman just by talking. But Mattie had also heard Slade's voice when it was as dangerous and cold as black ice.

"It's only fitting that I won tonight, Mattie," Doc said. "It's my birthday. I'm forty-seven years old today, and Lord knows I feel every one of those years."

"That's not old, Doc," Mattie said, smiling at the thin, good-looking man.

"It's getting there." He stood up. "I'm going to get us all a drink. We'll have a toast to me on my special day."

He walked away, and Slade began to stack his coins in front of him. "Trouble, Mattie?" he asked.

"How did you know?"

"I can tell."

She sat down next to him. "I need to talk to you, Slade, alone, as quickly as possible."

He nodded, then glanced up as Doc returned carrying three glasses.

"I didn't spill a drop," Doc said as he set the glasses on the table and sat down.

"Doc, I'm sorry," Mattie said. "I wasn't thinking. You shouldn't be paying for drinks on your birthday."

"True," Slade said. He picked up a few coins and tossed them into the pile in front of the doctor.

"I'll make the toast," Doc said, lifting his glass. Slade and Mattie lifted theirs too. "It's my birthday after all, so I can do as I please. I drink to you two, who I consider to be my closest . . . friends." He tipped his glass toward Slade, then slowly shifted his gaze to Mattie, looking directly into her green eyes. "To you, Mattie Muldoon."

"No," she said softly, "to you. It's your birthday, not mine. Happy birthday, Doc, and I hope you'll have many, many more."

Doc smiled. The trio sipped their whiskey, and Doc's gaze never left Mattie.

Slade glanced from Mattie to Doc, rolling the whiskey around on his tongue. Doc was in love with Mattie, he mused. He had suspected as much for a long time, but now was certain of it. Doc was making no attempt to conceal his feelings; love shone in his eyes. Mattie had to be able to see it, and Slade knew she would ignore it. Whatever she might feel for Doc Willis, she would never allow it to surface. She could never completely forgive herself for the life she'd led. Doc, to her, would always be out of her reach.

Slade swallowed more liquor. It took a helluva man, he realized, to do what Doc had done. He'd toasted Slade, calling him his friend, when he believed Slade was sleeping with the woman he loved. Doc Willis was a cut above the herd. And he and Mattie were still staring at each other.

The spell at the table was broken as a young cowboy rushed through the room, yelling Doc's name.

"There's been a helluva brawl at the Wooden Nickel," he gasped when he reached the table. "That fancy assistant doc you hired from back East said to come find you 'cause he's got more bloodied-up cowboys than he can handle. He's just a kid, that doc. You sure he knows what he's doin'?"

"He's older than you are, Tulsa," Doc said. He set his glass down and stood up. "You go on back and tell him I'm on my way."

"Yes, sir," Tulsa said, then took off at a run.

Doc smiled down at Mattie and Slade. "That ends my birthday celebration, but at least I shared it with good company while it lasted. I best get along and help patch up those roughnecks."

"Good night, Doc," Mattie said.

" 'Night," he said, then picked up his money and walked away.

Mattie clasped both hands around her glass and stared

into the amber liquid. "Don't say anything, Slade," she murmured. "I don't want to hear it. I saw how Doc looked at me. I know . . . I don't want to talk about it."

Slade took off his Stetson to run his hand through his hair, then settled the hat back on his head, pulling it low on his forehead so it cast a shadow over his features. He didn't say a word.

"Dear God, where is my mind?" Mattie exclaimed, pushing the glass away from her. "I have to talk to you, Slade. It's terribly important. I need your help and . . . Let's go upstairs."

Slade nodded and stood, scooping his money off the table. As Mattie started toward the stairs, Slade stopped at the bar and handed the money to the enormous black man behind it.

"I'll take care of it for you, Slade," the man said.

Slade made his way across the noisy, crowded room to where Mattie waited for him at the bottom of the wide staircase. With his arm circling her shoulders, they went up the stairs.

"Dammit, Abe," Clara, one of the saloon girls, said to the man behind the bar. "See that?"

"Mattie's got first claim on Slade Ironbow," Abe said. "You know that. Mattie is a very beautiful woman."

"I know it, Abe," Clara said, pouting, "but I don't have to like it. Slade hasn't come near me since he's been back. I wonder how long he'll be in Dodge this time?"

"There's no telling with Slade," Abe said, pouring a whiskey for a customer.

Clara sighed. "I know. You see him when you see him."

"Slade answers only to himself," Abe said. "Mattie understands that. There's nobody going to tame Slade Ironbow. Only a fool would try. You best go earn your keep, Clara."

"Yeah, I'm going," Clara muttered, and walked away with an exaggerated sway to her hips.

Abe watched as Mattie and Slade disappeared into Mattie's suite of rooms at the end of the hall upstairs.

"Nope," Abe said, wiping a wet spot off the gleaming bar, "nobody's going to tame Slade Ironbow."

Mattie and Slade passed through her small office, sparsely furnished with a desk, two chairs in front of it and a straight-backed one behind it, and a small safe against one wall. On the far side were hand-carved double doors, which Mattie opened with a key she took from her pocket.

Slade was one of the few people who had ever seen Mattie's living quarters, who knew they were much different from what most people expected of the owner of the Silver Spur. No bright, flashy colors or ornate furnishings decorated the sitting room or bedroom beyond.

Instead, Mattie had chosen pale rose and gray fabrics and wallpaper, and furniture made of shiny, dark mahogany. Small throw pillows edged in white eyelet decorated a rose velveteen settee. Elegant in their simplicity, evoking soothing calmness, the rooms could have been lifted from the home of any of the finest families in the country. Only one object was strangely out of place in the sitting room—a large, butter-soft leather chair. Slade's chair.

Mattie turned up the wicks on two oil lamps, then looked up to see Slade still standing just inside the closed doors.

"Drink?" she asked.

He shook his head, and crossed the room to his leather chair. Sitting in it, he placed his Stetson on a small table.

"Cigar?"

Again, Slade shook his head. He stretched out his long legs, crossed them at the ankle, then laced his hands loosely on his chest. Mattie began to pace the floor, and he watched her with half-closed eyes.

He presented the picture of a man totally relaxed, even almost asleep, but Mattie knew he was very much awake and following her every move. She also knew he wouldn't push her to speak, wouldn't insist that she tell him whatever was troubling her. Slade had the quiet patience of his Indian ancestors, and if Mattie chose to pace for an hour without saying a word, he would simply wait for an hour.

Mattie pressed her hands to her cold cheeks, drew a steadying breath, then sat down on the settee and looked at Slade. A minute ticked by in silence.

"Slade," she said finally, "you and I are the only ones who know how I came to own the Silver Spur ten years ago. You bought it, deeded it over to me, then advanced me the money to fix it up and make it the finest saloon in Dodge." Slade didn't move, nor acknowledge that he'd heard her. "I've paid you back every penny, and you know I'll be grateful to you for the rest of my life. I never understood why you chose me over all the other girls here. You've always just said you saw something in me that no one else did. Your friendship has been precious to me. I hope you realize that."

Slade didn't move or speak.

"Lord above," Mattie said, throwing up her hands, "there are times when your stoic Indian silence is maddening, Slade Ironbow."

He lifted one shoulder in a barely discernible shrug. "I know how you came to own the Spur, Mattie."

"All right, fine," she said, waving a dismissing hand. "What we've never talked about is how I came to be working here in the first place."

"That's not any of my business."

"Believe me, Slade, I'd prefer not to discuss it with you or anyone, but I have to now because I need your help." She paused. "I was raised by a drunken father back in Ohio. My mother ran off when I was just a little girl, and I was left with a bitter man who drowned his sorrows in a bottle. We lived in what was hardly more than a shack, and I cooked and cleaned and tried to please him. But he still drank, and when he did he beat me because I looked so much like my mother."

Slade remained silent, but Mattie saw a muscle jump along his jaw.

"I finally couldn't take it any longer," she went on, "and when a wagon train came through, I begged a family to take me with them. I offered to cook, do the wash, tend to the four children, if they'd give me food. They agreed, and I slipped away in the night to join them. I was barely sixteen then. It was a rough crossing, and a fever hit the wagon train. Two of the children died . . . It was horrible. When we got to Dodge, the family said they couldn't spare the food to take me farther. I was suddenly here, all alone, and terribly frightened."

She stopped speaking, as a shiver ripped through her, vivid pictures of her past flashing before her eyes. After a minute she had herself under control again, and lifted her chin as she continued.

"I met a young girl about my age, Maria Sanchez. She'd run away, too, from a life of poverty in Mexico. Maria and I lived in a tent at the edge of town and took in washing. Dodge was barely a town then, just mostly tents filled with trappers, gamblers, and prospectors hoping to strike it rich. Maria and I learned how to use a gun to protect ourselves from the men who came sniffing around our tent. Would you like a drink now?"

"No."

Mattie clasped her hands tightly in her lap and stared at her slender fingers. "Then I met a man. He was different from the others, so refined, a real gentleman. Or so I thought. He'd come calling and say I was the most beautiful girl he'd ever seen, an angel. I was swept off my feet. I'd tell Maria that everything was going to change, that I was going to marry him and I'd take her with me to my splendid new house."

She shook her head in self-disgust. "What a child I was. So naive and trusting, believing every word that man said to me. Then—then I knew I was carrying his child. I was thrilled, could hardly wait for him to come to the tent so I could tell him my glorious news."

Slade uncrossed his ankles, then crossed them in the opposite direction.

Mattie lifted her gaze from her hands to Slade's face. "He was furious. He slapped me hard across the face and told me I was nothing but trash. He'd never planned to marry me. He had only sweet-talked me to get me into his bed, and I'd ruined his good time by getting pregnant. He stalked out, and I never saw him again. I didn't know what to do. Maria was hysterical, so afraid we'd starve, and she didn't see how we were going to tend to a baby, too. Believe me, I didn't know, either, but it was my baby, and I was determined that nothing would happen to it. Oh, Slade, I don't know how to tell you why I need you so much right now without going through all this."

"Go on," he said quietly.

"Yes. Well, the months went by and I was sick a great deal of the time. It was cold and damp in the tent and I was trying to do my share of the laundry, but there wasn't enough food. I was so afraid for my baby. Maria started talking about working in one of the saloons, and I begged her not to. She was so young and innocent, I knew that life would kill her. My time was coming near, and I honestly didn't know how I was going to take proper care of my child."

She abruptly stood up and began pacing the room again.

"I had a baby girl," she said softly, stopping in front of Slade. "Maria helped with the birthing, and I held my beautiful baby girl in my arms. And I cried because I was so frightened, so afraid my baby would never survive. And then . . . then he came. Jed Colten. He was with a wagon train on its way to Texas. He'd pulled out of the train in Dodge because his wife Bonnie was expecting a baby and was very sick. My own child was a week old when Mr. Colten came to see me. He'd heard about me, he said, and wanted to talk. He was young and strong, and as he spoke, he started crying. His wife had given birth to a girl, but the baby had died. Bonnie was in a fever, and didn't know her baby was dead. Slade, Jed Colten was the kindest, gentlest man I'd ever met. His Bonnie was his life, his reason for living."

Unnoticed tears spilled onto Mattie's cheeks as she sank back down on the settee. "He said it would break his wife's heart when she learned their baby had died. He swore on all that was holy that he'd give my daughter a good life, treat her as his own if I'd let him. No one would ever know, especially Bonnie, that the child wasn't a Colten. I knew in my heart that I owed my baby a chance at a life better than I could provide for her. Jed wanted to give me money, but I refused. My only demand was that he take Maria with him, get her out of Dodge, let her be a part of his household. I swore I would never try to see my daughter if he'd take Maria. Slade, I—I gave my baby to Jed Colten. Do you hate me for that?"

"No."

"I gave my baby away!"

Slade straightened in the chair and leaned forward, resting his elbows on his knees.

"No," he said, looking directly at her, "you gave your baby a *chance*. That took more courage and love than keeping her."

"Thank you," Mattie said, dashing her tears away. "Mr. Colten took the baby and Maria. My life got worse in Dodge, until I was nearly starving. I just gave up and went to work at the Silver Spur. It was rough, sometimes frightening. Fistfights—gunfights every night, and the other women were so hard, so completely without hope. I just blanked my mind and did what I had to do. Each day, each night, I thought about my daughter.

"Over the years, Maria has sent me letters whenever she knew of someone who was coming to Dodge City. She felt I'd saved her life, and to repay me she kept me informed about my child. Jed Colten did well in Texas. He homesteaded, then bought up neighboring land as people gave up on it. He named his spread the Bonnie Blue. They named my daughter Becca. When Becca was six, Bonnie died of pneumonia. Maria assured me that the Bonnie Blue was a wonderful ranch, that Jed Colten was devoted to Becca, and that with Maria's help he would raise her. He never remarried, because his only love had been Bonnie, and he centered his attention on Becca. To him, she was his own daughter, and I found peace in that."

"You should," Slade said. "You did the right thing, Mattie."

"But, Slade, now there's trouble, terrible trouble, and I need your help. I've had a letter from Maria. Jed Colten was killed two months ago when his horse threw him. Becca has just turned twenty-one and inherited the Bonnie Blue. But another rancher, Henry Folger, is trying to get the ranch. Maria said he offered to marry Becca, but Becca refused. Folger was livid, and threatened to get the Bonnie Blue any way he could. Maria is frightened for Becca, and Becca is determined to stand her ground and run the ranch herself. Oh, Slade, I'm so afraid for my baby."

"Where's the Bonnie Blue?" he asked.

"In the northwest section of the Texas Panhandle, just over the border below Oklahoma. Three, maybe four days' hard ride from here."

Slade planted his large hands on his thighs and pushed himself to his feet. "I'll leave at dawn."

Mattie jumped up and grasped his hands, tears filling her eyes again.

"You'll help her? You'll help Becca?" she asked, a sob choking her voice.

"You knew I would."

"It could be dangerous, Slade. It doesn't sound like Henry Folger will take kindly to anyone getting in his way. I hate to ask this of you, but I didn't know where else to turn."

"I'm the only one you should have come to with this. You know that, too."

"Becca mustn't know about me."

"I understand."

"You can tell Maria who you are but . . . how will you explain yourself to Becca?"

"I'll think of something once I get there and see the situation. Try not to worry. I'll send word to you when I can."

Mattie wrapped her arms around his waist and leaned her head on his chest. He embraced her, holding her tightly to him.

"There aren't words to thank you," she said, sobbing openly. "I love you, my friend. How can I ever repay you?"

He gripped her upper arms and set her away from him. "You can stop crying. I've never seen you with tears in your eyes before, Mattie, and I don't know what to do with a crying woman."

She managed a small smile and swept the tears from her cheeks. "There. No more tears. But, Slade, please be careful. Maria says that Henry Folger is rich and powerful, and will stop at nothing to get the Bonnie Blue. I'll never forgive myself if anything happens to you. If it weren't for Becca being in danger . . . Oh, promise me you'll be on your guard."

He picked his Stetson up. "I will," he said as he settled his hat low on his forehead. "Don't expect to hear from me right off. Put your mind on something else if you can." He started toward the door. "For instance, you could think about Doc Willis and the fact that he's in love with you. And that maybe it's time Doc knew that you and I aren't doing up here what everyone thinks we are."

"Slade, don't be ridiculous. Doc is a fine, upstanding citizen of Dodge City."

Slade put his hand on the doorknob, then turned to look at her. "So are you."

"No, I'm not. I don't want to talk about Doc. My thoughts will be with you and Becca. My prayers, too. Please be—"

"Careful. I always am. I'm going to get some sleep. I've got a hard ride ahead of me. Good night."

"Good night, and I thank you with all my heart."

Slade nodded, then left the room, closing the door with a quiet click.

Mattie's trembling legs refused to hold her for another moment, and she sank onto the leather chair. She could feel the comforting warmth from Slade's body. As another sob rose in her throat, she gave up the battle against her emotions. It had been many years since she'd cried, and now she seemed unable to stop the flow of tears.

She covered her face with her hands and wept.

Two

Slade slowly walked down the stairs and out of the Silver Spur. Clara stamped her foot in a fit of temper, causing Abe to chuckle and shake his head.

Outside, Slade glanced around instinctively to take stock of the mood of the city. Saturday nights were usually wild and reckless. The numerous saloons were ablaze with light, music and raucous laughter pouring out of them in waves.

The sheriff and all his deputies would be keeping careful watch, Slade knew. Sunday morning, cowboys would be waking with aching heads and foggy memories. Some would be battered and bruised, others would find themselves in jail and wonder how they'd gotten there.

The church would be packed for the weekly service, and the preacher would forcefully denounce the evils of drink and the sins of the flesh. Monday would bring a return of the work routine, then next Saturday night the process would begin all over again.

Slade strode along the weatherworn wooden planks laid as sidewalks above the dusty streets, Becca Colten's name ringing in his mind. Mattie's daughter. Mattie's secret for twenty-one years. What it must have taken, he thought, for her to give up her baby. She was strong, his Mattie, and her heart and soul were purer than those of the many hypocrites who'd show up at church the next morning.

He'd sensed the goodness in Mattie the first time he'd seen her, and had set about to make a better life for her. Mattie was one of the few people he allowed to get close to him. He'd never touched her as a lover. She was his friend, pure and simple.

As Slade strolled toward the hotel he stayed in whenever he was in town, he saw Doc Willis sitting on the bench in front of his office on the other side of the street. Slade crossed the street, kicking up dust, and settled onto the bench next to the doctor. Several minutes passed in silence.

"You're turning in early," Doc finally said.

"Yep."

"I just fixed up some battered cowpokes. God knows why, but those poor buzzards inspired me to take stock of my life. You ever do that, Slade? You ever sit on a bench and take stock of your life?"

"No."

"Well, maybe it's because it's my birthday. A man sometimes takes a hard look at himself on his birthday."

"Sometimes."

"Can't say I liked what I came up with."

"No?"

"No. I'm a lonely man, Slade. I want a wife, a family, before I'm too old to have one."

"Reasonable."

"No, it's not, because the woman I love belongs to someone else. Can't see myself settling for less."

"No."

Doc chuckled. "Carrying on a conversation with you is like talking to a board. Never met a man who can say so much with so few words the way you do. I suppose that's the Indian part of you coming through."

"Yep."

"What would you do, Slade, if the woman you loved belonged to another man? Not married, mind you. He's just staked his claim on her."

"Shoot him."

Doc shook his head. "Oh, hell."

"You asked."

"All right. Suppose this man you're planning on shooting is a friend of yours? What then?"

"Depends on how much I want her."

"Love her. There's a big difference between wanting and loving."

"I wouldn't know."

"You've never been in love?"

"No."

"You ever killed a man because you wanted his woman?"

"No."

"I couldn't do it."

"I know you couldn't, Doc. And it isn't even necessary. Mattie and I aren't lovers, never have been. You are now the only other person who knows that. Because everyone believes she's mine, men stay away from her. That's what she wants. I know you love her; I've known for a long time. I figure you're about to do something about it. Don't feel you have to shoot me, though."

Doc shook his head again.

"I can't believe this."

"Believe it."

"Slade, before you go back to your short Indian answers, could you tell me how I'm going to convince Mattie Muldoon to marry me? I'm not even sure she likes me much."

"She likes you."

"She does?"

"Yes. She likes you just fine. The problem, Doc, is that Mattie doesn't carry a real high opinion of herself. With you being a respectable doctor, a high-class citizen and all . . ." Slade's voice trailed off, and he shrugged.

"Lord, when you start talking, you really have things to say. Mattie doesn't think she's good enough for me? That's pure horse manure. I'd be the proudest man alive to have her as my wife."

"Tell her."

"Oh, Lord," Doc said, looking to the heavens.

"Doc, I'm riding out at dawn to tend to some business. Mattie's a bit upset about a private matter, and I'd appreciate your checking on her for me. When I'm a day's ride out and she can't come gun me down, tell her I told you the truth about her and me. The rest is up to you."

"You've said more tonight than you've said in the past ten years."

Slade got to his feet. "You'll wait ten more years to hear as much again. I'm all worn out. 'Night, Doc."

"Thank you, Slade. I count myself lucky to have you for a friend. You realize, don't you, that if I start courting Mattie while you're gone, everyone will expect you to come back and shoot me dead as a post?"

Slade chuckled. "That they will. There will be lots of disappointed folks around here. They do enjoy a good shooting. Do you mind if I get some sleep now?"

"Oh, sorry. Good night, Slade, and thanks again."

"Happy birthday," Slade said, then disappeared silently into the darkness.

"It wasn't a happy birthday," Doc said to no one, a smile creeping onto his face, "until now."

A half-day's ride out of Dodge, Slade left the well-traveled road and headed for the backcountry. He had no desire to meet up with the various travelers, salesmen, down-on-their-luck cowboys, and thieves who traversed the better-known thoroughfares. He always felt more comfortable finding his way in uncharted territory. There his sixth sense would warn him of any danger from man or beast or terrain.

Blanking his mind of thought, beyond listening for potential trouble, he rode tirelessly. His horse, a big, black stallion, knew every nuance of his master's body, and the two moved nearly as one entity, emanating gracefulness and seemingly unending power and strength. The wind accompanied them, as though realizing this man and beast were kin, as fleet and wild as itself.

For Slade it was a cleansing time away from the noise and activity of Dodge City. He filled his lungs with the whipping wind and pushed on. At dusk he found a secluded spot to make camp. After tending to the needs of his horse, he stripped bare and plunged into a swirling stream that washed away the dust of his hard ride.

His food was simple but nourishing, and included pecans from the many trees that grew near the water. Tall oak and elm trees stood like proud sentries at the edge of the stark desert beyond, where the water couldn't reach.

When Slade slept, he slept light, his gun close to his side. At dawn he was up, cleanly shaven, dressed, fed, and saddling his horse, who pranced in anticipation of another day racing the wind.

He continued south, and could often see in the distance railroad tracks snaking across the land. Soon, he knew, the country would meet itself coming and going. What had been wild, would be tamed; what had been undiscovered, found. Among the men who ventured far into the West, some were pure of heart, carrying hopes and dreams for a better life. Others were simply greedy, not caring about the land or its natural gifts as they took all they could for themselves, then moved on.

It was a time of change, and Slade accepted that, as did his father's people. The Indians had fought bravely to hold what had always been theirs. Fought and lost. Most of the tribes now lived on reservations, scratching out an existence far different from their fathers' before them.

As time passed, though, Indians were slowly gaining nervous acceptance in the towns, where they bought supplies. In his many travels, Slade had seen Indian children sitting next to white in small schoolhouses; seen on occasion a white man tip his hat to a young Indian woman in the marketplace.

Perhaps, his father often said, there would be a time of total peace in the country, with all people living side by side with no thought of color, creed, or heritage. Perhaps, Slade always answered, but he felt in his heart that it would never come to be.

Man was a creature of fear, and what he didn't understand he struck out at. Until that changed, there would be dissension. But for now, at least, a tentative calm held as everyone struggled to survive.

In the late afternoon, three days after leaving Dodge, Slade sat on his horse on a rise high above the sprawling Bonnie Blue ranch.

Early in the day he'd met an old prospector with no particular destination in mind who was riding along on a mule. The man knew the Bonnie Blue and told Slade exactly how to find it. It was the finest spread around, stretching for miles in every direction, the old man had said, though Lord knew what was to become of it with Jed Colten dead.

"Second best is Folger's place," the man said. "Four Aces, he calls it." He spat tobacco juice on the ground. "Big spread, right next to the Bonnie Blue. Folger wants Colten's land real bad, I hear. Put them two ranches together, he'd be takin' a big bite out of Texas soil. Can't say I know how it's all goin' to end up, but I'm headin' out. Texas is gettin' too crowded for me."

Slade had nodded, then pressed on to find the Colten ranch. Gazing at it at last, he knew it was all he had heard about it.

Cattle covered the rich, rolling, checkerboard land. Some acreage was lush, with alfalfa growing tall and thick. Other sections had been well grazed, and were left alone now to replenish their bounty. Dozens of horses nibbled grass and raced in large fenced-off enclosures. In the distance were buildings—a huge barn, sheds, a bunkhouse, and a sprawling ranch house.

The Bonnie Blue was a fine spread, he thought, one of the best he'd seen. Windmills were pumping the precious water needed to keep it all going. He could see cowboys leading horses into the barn; smoke curled up from the chimneys of the bunkhouse and ranch house, indicating supper was being prepared. A sense of peace enveloped the scene, a sense of man and nature working together to create harmony.

But just how peaceful was it? Slade wondered. Had Maria Sanchez panicked when she'd sent the message to Mattie? Did Becca Colten intend to marry Henry Folger and merge the two ranches, but put the man through his paces first?

The Bonnie Blue was enormous. That meant money. Jed Colten had adored his adopted daughter, treated her as his own flesh and blood. That could have produced one very pampered and spoiled young lady, whose act of defiance was nothing more than a display of female dramatics. Or was Becca really in danger, as Mattie feared?

There was, Slade thought dryly, only one way to find out, and sitting up there on a hill admiring the Bonnie Blue wasn't going to get him the answers he needed.

He swung his horse around and made his way back

down the rise, deciding to approach the ranch from the front. If he was riding into a hornet's nest, he preferred to face it head-on. If nothing was really wrong, he'd be on his way before heavy darkness fell.

Nearly an hour later, Slade had made his way down, then around the miles of fenced land, which were even richer and more fertile at close view. At last he followed a winding dirt road that led to the gleaming white house. He walked his horse at an easy pace, his gaze flicking in all directions. He saw no one.

Stopping in front of the house, he saw it was well cared for. Two stories high and painted a sparkling white, it had a sweeping front porch, reminding him of a plantation house he'd seen when traveling through the South a few years earlier. As he prepared to dismount, the front door burst open.

Slade stiffened when he saw a rifle pointed at his chest. And holding that rifle, stepping slowly onto the porch, was one of the most beautiful women he'd ever seen.

This was Becca. She was dressed in mourning black, and her auburn hair, darker than Mattie's, was pulled back. She'd inherited Mattie's green eyes and creamy complexion, but she wasn't Mattie. She was Becca, uniquely herself. Tall and full-breasted, with a tiny waist and slim hips. Her features were delicate and lovely; her lips inspired dreams of stolen kisses on moonlit nights. Yes, Becca Colten was beautiful, and at the moment she was ready to shoot him dead.

"Ma'am," he said, touching two fingers to the brim of his Stetson.

"Just turn around and leave, mister," she said. "I know Folger sent you. I don't have any idea what his plan is this time, but you can tell him that the Bonnie Blue is not for sale, and neither am I. Now, move it."

"Before you pull that trigger," Slade said, "I might just mention that I don't know anyone named Folger."

"Who are you?"

Before Slade could reply, the sound of rapidly approaching horses snapped Becca's head up. Four riders galloped up to the house, and Becca shifted the rifle from Slade to them. Slade sat perfectly still, giving the appearance of being completely relaxed. The men pulled their horses to a stop, glanced at Slade, then looked at Becca.

"Howdy, ma'am," one said. "Just came checking on you for Mr. Folger. He's mighty concerned about you, you know, being over here on your own."

"In a pig's eye," Becca said. "You're not welcome on Bonnie Blue land, any of you, including Folger. You tell him that—again—and maybe one of these days it will sink into his thick skull."

Slade watched her with surprise and admiration. Her eyes glittered with anger, and her breasts rose and fell rapidly. He'd seen her pale as the men approached, but she was standing her ground. The trembling of the rifle was barely discernible. Becca Colten wasn't playing games. This was no show of female dramatics. She was most definitely in trouble.

"Now, now, Miss Colten," the man said, almost sneering, "that ain't real neighborly of you. Mr. Folger's just worried about you, is all. It's bad enough your pa had the fall that killed him, and now we hear tell over at Four Aces your foreman met with a real unfortunate accident. Broke his leg, is how the story goes. So, Mr. Folger, being a gentleman and all, sent me to take his place. I brought some of my boys along to help out. My name is Casey, and I'm at your service, ma'am. Your new foreman."

"She already *has* a new foreman," Slade said quietly, shifting his gaze to the four men.

They turned their heads around to look at him. Becca stared at him, too, her eyes wide.

"Who in the hell are you?" Casey asked.

"Just told you," Slade said. "The foreman."

"You got a name?"

"Yep."

"So?" Casey said. "What is it?"

"Miss Colten knows who I am," Slade said. "You don't need to."

"Who is this man?" Casey asked Becca. "We didn't hear nothin' about your hirin' a new foreman."

"Because it's none of your business," Becca said. "Now, turn those horses around and get off my land."

"Not 'til we got a name to take back to Folger," Casey said. "He's going to want to know who you brought in."

"Ironbow," Slade said. "Slade Ironbow. I'm only telling you because you're making Miss Colten and me late for supper."

"Holy hell, Casey," one of the other men whispered. "Did you hear him? He's Slade Ironbow. I've heard about him. All kinds of things. Let's get the hell out of here."

"I ain't afraid of you, Ironbow!" Casey yelled.

Slade shrugged. "You should be, but it's up to you. You can leave upright in the saddle, or slung over it. Take your pick."

"On your way," Becca said, tightening her hold on the rifle.

Casey hesitated, glaring at Slade, then looked back at Becca.

"Folger isn't going to like this," he said, "your bringin' in a fast gun. Folger's been keeping this nice and friendly, but you're changin' the rules."

"Folger's idea of friendly doesn't match mine," she said. "Nothing he's done has come close to being friendly. Don't come back, any of you. I'll say this one last time. The Bonnie Blue is not for sale, and neither am I. Go!"

"Now," Slade added quietly.

With a muttered curse, Casey swung his horse around and galloped off, the others right behind him. Becca slowly lowered the rifle, drew in a shuddering breath as she watched them leave in the billowing dust, then swallowed hard.

Slade waited, not moving, for her to regain control. She had, he realized, momentarily forgotten he was there as the shock of the encounter with Folger's men took its toll. She suddenly seemed fragile, vulnerable, and he fought the urge to go to her and pull her into his arms, to tell her no harm would come to her because he was with her now.

Nothing, he vowed, was going to happen to the Bonnie Blue or to Becca Colten. He'd protect her. Tears should never cloud her eyes as they did now; her lower lip shouldn't tremble with fear and despair. No, he'd take care—

Slade drew himself up short, stunned by his thoughts. What he was thinking, and feeling, had nothing to do with his friendship with Mattie. Becca was rousing powerful emotions in him, not because she needed his help, but because she was a beautiful, desirable woman. And those powerful emotions threatened the control he always maintained.

"Could I get off this horse now?" he asked gruffly. "Assuming you've decided not to shoot me."

Becca blinked, then spun around to face him. She'd unconsciously cradled the rifle, pointing it harmlessly at the ground. "What? Oh, yes, of course . . ."

Slade swung from the saddle in a smooth, graceful motion. The reins in one hand, he shoved his Stetson up with his thumb and gazed at her. Their eyes met, and he felt a coil of heat tighten deep within him.

Damn, he thought, what was it about this woman? She was turning him inside out just looking at him. He was hungry, that was it. He'd had a long day in the saddle, and a decent meal and a night's sleep would chase away these unsettling reactions to her.

"Who are you?" she asked. "I know your name is Slade

Ironbow, and Folger's men said you were a fast gun. They were obviously intimidated by you. What are you doing here on the Bonnie Blue, Mr. Ironbow?" She lifted her chin, steadily holding his gaze.

Well, Slade thought dryly, Miss Colten was definitely back in control. "Hear tell it, I'm your new foreman."

"Look, Mr. Ironbow—"

"Slade."

"I believe, sir," she said stiffly, "that you owe me an explanation for your presence on the Bonnie Blue."

He shook his head. "Now you're getting all snooty. You do change moods right quickly, Miss Colten."

"Answer my question," Becca said, her voice rising. "How do I know this whole thing wasn't staged? How do I know you don't really work for Henry Folger, and this isn't a carefully concocted plan of his? Just how do I know that, Mr. Ironbow?"

"Slade."

Anger flashed in her eyes once more. "Damn you."

A smile tugged at the corner of Slade's mouth, then was gone. "Now you're swearing like a drunken cowboy. You're an amazing woman, Miss Colten." She really was, he thought. She was fire and fury one minute, then looked like a frightened fawn the next. She'd be a lot to handle for any man who tried to stake a claim on her, make her his.

"I need to see to my horse," he said, cutting off his musings before they went down the wrong road again. "We've had a long, hard ride. Then, if you can spare me a plate of supper, I'll answer your questions."

Before Becca could reply, a young cowboy raced around the side of the house. He pulled up short when he saw Slade.

"Miss Becca?" he asked, his gaze darting back and forth between her and Slade. "Are you all right? I saw dust from the road. Were Folger's men here?"

"Yes, they were," Becca said, "but I'm fine. Bucky, would you please see to Mr. Ironbow's horse? Mr. Ironbow and I have things to discuss."

"Yes, ma'am," Bucky said. He approached Slade cautiously. "I'll feed and water him, brush him down real good. Fine animal, sir. A beauty."

Slade lifted his saddlebags off the horse and flung them over one shoulder, then handed the reins to Bucky.

"Horse got a name?" Bucky asked.

"No," Slade said.

"Oh. Well, I'll tend to him just fine. Good evening, Miss Becca."

"Thank you, Bucky," she said, watching as he led the horse away. Then she switched her gaze back to Slade.

"I need to wash up," he said, and added, "before supper."

Her mouth tightened. "All right, Mr. Ironbow, you win. For now. There's a pump around back where you can wash up. Come into the house through the kitchen door when you're finished. I'll tell Maria to set an extra place for supper. During supper—not after—I'll expect you to answer my questions."

He nodded and started away. "Slade," he said over his shoulder without breaking his long-legged stride.

Becca glared at his retreating back, then went into the house, slamming the door behind her. After setting the rifle back in a rack that held six others, she strode down the long hallway to the kitchen.

Was she making a mistake by letting Slade Ironbow into her home? she asked herself. What if he was one of Folger's men? Casey and the others could have pretended to be frightened of him. Mr. Ironbow had better have some straight answers for her. But how was she to know if he was telling her the truth? Oh, saints above, she was about to have supper with a gunfighter!

She entered the kitchen to find Maria looking out the window.

"Maria, would you please set an extra place for supper? Mr. Ironbow will be joining me."

Maria glanced at Becca, then turned back to the window. She was a short, plump woman, with dark hair pulled into a neat bun, and warm, expressive brown eyes. While not beautiful, Maria had an aura about her that made one immediately feel comfortable with her.

"Is that your Mr. Ironbow washing up there?" Maria asked. "Mercy, mercy, mercy, that is one fine-looking man. He took his shirt off to wash up and his chest, his back, his arms . . . Muscles in all the right places and skin like polished copper. Mercy, mercy—"

"Maria, for heaven's sake," Becca said, "you've seen many a man wash up for supper."

"Not one like that," Maria said, her gaze still riveted on Slade. "Where'd he come from, Becca?"

"I don't know." Do not look out that window, Becca Colten, she told herself firmly. "I intend to get answers to my questions over supper." She moved closer to Maria, and of its own volition, it seemed, her gaze was drawn to the window. "Oh. Oh, my," she said softly.

Slade was just reaching for his shirt, and the muscles in his back rippled beneath taut, bronzed skin. He turned to shrug into the dark shirt, and Becca's breath caught in her throat as she saw the moist, black hair on his chest. A funny flutter danced along her spine; her cheeks warmed.

"Got some Indian in him by the looks of him," Maria said. "Name sounds Indian. But he's part white, too, 'cause he's got hair on his chest. Oh, he is a handsome devil, that one."

"He's a gunfighter," Becca said.

Maria shrugged. "I knew that right off. You can tell from the way he wears that gun low on his hips and tied down. You don't know where he came from, or why he's here?"

"No," Becca said, "but I'll know before supper is over. Four of Folger's men were here. Slade—Mr. Ironbow told them he was my new foreman. As soon as he said his name, the Four Aces men hightailed it down the road."

Maria laughed. "I'm sorry I missed seeing that. So, your Slade has a reputation, does he?"

"Maria, he's not mine." Becca spun around. "I'll wash up in my room. Please ask Mr. Ironbow to meet me in the dining room."

"That I will," Maria said as Becca stalked out of the kitchen. "But if I don't quit gawking at the man, there won't be any supper to serve up."

As Maria returned to the large wood-burning stove, the back door opened and Slade walked in, carrying his Stetson and saddlebags. He set them on the floor next to the door. Maria turned and smiled at him.

"Welcome to the Bonnie Blue, Mr. Ironbow. I'm Maria Sanchez, the housekeeper."

"It's Slade."

"Well, then, you call me Maria, Slade. Supper will be on in just a few minutes. Becca said to go into the dining room. It's down the hall, first door on the right."

"Where's Becca?"

"In her room washing up."

Slade nodded and crossed the kitchen to stand in front of Maria. "Mattie sent me," he said quietly.

"Oh, praise the Lord," Maria said, covering her heart with her hand. "We're in trouble here, Slade. Bad trouble. I hated to upset Mattie, but I didn't know what else to do. Do you know that Becca . . . that is . . ."

"I know that Becca is Mattie's daughter. Mattie and I are close friends."

"Just friends?"

"Yes."

"Interesting," Maria said. "Anyway, Slade, Becca must never know who her real mother is."

"I understand that. She won't hear it from me."

"Slade, my Becca—I love her as though she were my own—has been through so much these past weeks. Jed's dying was a shock to us all, but Becca is taking it so hard. She was very close to her pa, and he thought the sun rose and set because she wished it. Jed was hardly a month in his grave when Henry Folger came courting Becca. Folger, that swine, wants the Bonnie Blue, and he'll do anything to get it. I'm glad you're here. Becca needs you. We all do."

"I have to convince *her* of that. She definitely has a mind of her own."

"She's feisty, that's for sure, and brave, and . . . well, she's Becca. She won't give up the Bonnie Blue without a hard fight, Slade, and I'm frightened for her." She paused and glanced toward the door. "You best get to the dining room. You and I will talk again later. I do praise the Lord that you're here. I knew Mattie would know what to do. You just stand your ground and tell Becca you're staying. Oh, mercy, she's liable to throw a fit of temper."

Slade chuckled. "Wouldn't surprise me at all. I'll speak with you again when I can."

As Slade left the kitchen, Maria clasped her hands together and looked heavenward for a long moment, then returned to the stove nodding decisively.

Three

In her room, Becca washed her face and hands in the large china bowl on her dresser, then undid the black ribbon that held her hair back. The heavy, auburn tresses fell in waves halfway down her back. She brushed her hair and retied the ribbon, then glanced at her reflection in the oval mirror above the dresser. Her eyes revealed a familiar, lingering sadness, as she'd known they would, along with fatigue.

She braced her hands on the dresser and leaned closer, peering at her image. There was something else there in her eyes, she realized, a flicker of brightness, and her cheeks had a rosy glow.

The memory of Slade standing by the pump without his shirt flitted through her mind, and she frowned as she felt again the funny flutter along her spine, as well as a strange heat that pulsed within her.

She was acting like a child who'd never seen a handsome man before, she admonished herself. She'd grown up surrounded by men on the Bonnie Blue, and had always been comfortable around them. She enjoyed their company, and had spent many pleasant afternoons and evenings with young men from neighboring ranches. No, men were not strangers to her.

Yet . . .

She turned from the mirror and smoothed her dress over her hips. Yes, she admitted to herself, Slade Ironbow was very different from any other man she'd ever met.

Power and strength emanated from him, and a nearly tangible essence of virility and masculinity. Good-looking? Yes. Well-built? Yes. Dangerous? Very.

He had an incredible voice, she mused. And eyes. They were as dark as coal, and had seemed to look right through her dress to her heated skin. Who was he, this man who evoked such new and strange sensations within her? What was he doing on the Bonnie Blue?

Well, she intended to find out exactly who he was and why he was there. She would eat supper with the mysterious Mr. Ironbow, and if his answers left any niggling doubts in her mind that he might be working for Henry Folger, she'd send Slade Ironbow packing.

Becca squared her shoulders, lifted her chin, and left the bedroom. As she neared the dining room, she told herself the fluttering butterflies in her stomach and the trembling in her knees were solely because of hunger.

When Slade had entered the dining room and discovered Becca was not yet there, he'd wandered down the hall to the large living room. Glancing around, he was struck immediately by the welcoming atmosphere of the room.

Richly decorated with massive dark wood furniture and earth colors, with a huge stone fireplace covering nearly one entire wall, the room spoke of the rugged West, of Texas, and a man who had taken great pride in what he possessed. While the decor had a definite masculine flair, Slade had no difficulty picturing Becca Colten in the room.

He'd seen her passion as fury when she'd faced him and the men from Four Aces. What if that passion turned to desire? What if it were directed at him, and he took her into his arms and loved her? It would be, he knew, a magnificent joining, unlike anything he'd experienced before.

"Mr. Ironbow," Becca said from the doorway, "you weren't in the dining room. Maria is putting supper on now, if you'd care to join me."

He turned to face her. "Slade."

She inclined her head. "Slade. Shall we go?" She turned with a swish of dark skirt and disappeared.

Slade chuckled as he followed her from the room. "Snooty again."

A glittering chandelier ablaze with candles lighted the dining room. Becca seated herself at the end of a gleaming cherry-wood table that was at least ten feet long. She sat, Slade surmised, in the chair that had been her father's, making it clear *she* was now owner of the Bonnie Blue.

Maria was putting platters of food on the table—roast beef, potatoes, beans, and biscuits. Another place was set directly to Becca's right. Slade crossed the room to his chair. Becca didn't look at him.

"Would you consider removing your gun while we eat?" she asked.

"No," he said, sitting down.

Maria laughed. "You asked, you got an answer, Becca. Now then, you two dig right in there. And you see that you eat plenty, Becca Colten. You're wasting away to nothing more than a little bird." With that, Maria bustled out of the room.

A fragile little bird, Slade thought, easily frightened and hurt. Well, not while he was there.

"Help yourself," Becca said, lifting a slice of roast beef onto her plate.

He wanted her, Slade thought suddenly. He wanted to touch her cheek to see if her skin was as soft as it appeared. He wanted to pull the ribbon from her hair and weave his fingers through the heavy, silken locks, watch them float over her breasts, her bare breasts. He wanted to nestle her to him, kiss her tempting lips, then lower her to a bed . . .

As Slade's body tightened from his unexpected wayward thoughts, he cleared his throat roughly and filled his plate with the steaming food. They ate in silence for several minutes.

He had very refined table manners, Becca thought, watching Slade from beneath her lashes. He was no stranger to dining at elegant tables. Women probably often invited him to join them for a meal. And to join them in bed? Probably.

Becca stiffened. Shame on you, she scolded herself. She'd never before entertained such wanton thoughts concerning a man and a bed. Never.

It was one thing to stand on her front porch, rifle in hand, and square off against the formidable Mr. Ironbow. It was quite another to be alone with him in the somewhat intimate atmosphere of two people sharing supper. Shouldn't Maria be hovering around, acting as a chaperone of sorts?

Becca took a sip of coffee and told herself to calm down. There was, after all, a definite purpose to her having supper with Slade. It was vitally important that she learn why he had suddenly arrived at the Bonnie Blue.

But how could she even think when he was somehow filling the room to overflowing with his vibrant, masculine presence? He was just so male, and just so there, and she didn't seem able to draw enough air into her lungs.

"Mr. . . . Slade, suppose we get down to business," she said, hoping her voice was steady. "Why are you here? And, please, don't say that you're my new foreman."

"I *am* your new foreman," he said.

"No, you are not," she said stiffly. "I don't even know who you are, how you happened to appear on my land. I'm not convinced you're not working for Folger."

"Never met the man." Slade finished his potatoes and piled more on his plate.

"You just happened by accidentally?"

"No."

"Damn it," she exclaimed, "would you give me some straight answers?"

"Swearing like a drunken cowboy again. Ladies aren't supposed to swear, Miss Colten."

"I'm warning you, Slade Ironbow, I've had enough of this. You tell me what I want to know, or saddle up and ride out of here."

Slade took a deep swallow of coffee, carefully replaced the china cup in the saucer, then looked directly at her.

"I'm here," he said quietly, "because you're in trouble, and you need me to be here. I'm going to be your foreman because it's the best way to handle this."

"But I don't even know you. Why would I or the Bonnie Blue matter to you?"

"Let's just say I owe a debt to your father."

"My father? You knew him?"

"Not directly. He did a kind thing for someone I know who can't repay the favor. *I* can. I intend to."

"I'm to understand that you're acting on someone else's behalf? Repaying an act of kindness my father showed this other person?"

"Close enough."

"Why?" she asked, leaning toward him. "Why would you do that?"

He shrugged. "The person asked me to."

"You'd walk into a potentially dangerous situation involving people you don't even know because someone asked you to?"

"Yes."

Becca sat back in her chair and stared at him. "That's crazy."

"No." He took a bite of potatoes.

"Henry Folger is determined to get this ranch. You could be hurt, even killed, repaying a debt that isn't yours."

"I wasn't planning on getting myself killed."

She pounded her fist once on the table in frustration. "You may not have any say in the matter!"

"I generally have an opinion about living or dying, Miss Colten. So far, I've picked living. How many men do you have working for you?"

"Thirty-five, give or take a few."

"Do you know them all? Trust them?"

"I know most of them, and they've sworn their loyalty to me. Ten, maybe a dozen, are drifters who haven't been here very long."

"How did your foreman break his leg?"

"His horse threw him. Just—just the way my father's did. My pa was an excellent rider, and was on his own mount when it happened. The same holds true for Frank, the foreman. I find it hard to believe . . ." Her voice trailed off.

"That they were accidents? Miss Colten . . . Becca, do you think your father was purposely killed? Murdered by Henry Folger?"

"Yes," she whispered, fighting back sudden tears. "Yes, I do. I also think Frank was gotten out of the way deliberately too." She shook her head violently. "But how? No shots were heard to spook those horses. They were fine, then the next moment they went down. My father . . . my father struck his head on a rock and died instantly.

Frank's leg was broken three days ago. He's in the bunk-house with wooden splints on his leg, and he's in terrible pain. He said he can't figure out what happened. His horse just seemed to crumble beneath him, and he was thrown. He—Why am I telling you all this?"

"I have to know. I have to have a clear picture of things. Who's acting as foreman now?"

"Yancey Perkins. He's been here for years. He's worried, though; says he's too old to handle the job. There have been other incidents, too, in the past month. A mile of fence was cut, one of the steam-operated pumps we were using to irrigate a far section that had gone dry was destroyed, a natural water hole was polluted. All the men are getting nervous, wondering what Folger is going to do next."

Slade nodded. "Nervous men make mistakes. In the morning you can introduce me as the new foreman, and I'll take it from there."

"You certainly will not," she said, sitting bolt upright.

"Yes, I will."

"This is my ranch, Mr. Ironbow."

He sighed. "I don't doubt that you'll remind me of that every two minutes . . . ma'am. All right, I'll report in to you, tell you everything that I'm doing, what I see, what I think. That suit you?"

"I never agreed to your being the foreman."

"Do you have a better idea?"

"How do I know I can trust you?" she asked, leaning toward him again. "Answer that one. Just how in heaven's name do I know that I can trust you?"

"Becca," he said, looking directly into her eyes, "you can trust me."

Becca met his gaze, her heart racing. Slade's voice had seemed to drop an octave, and she was pinned in place by the fathomless depths of his dark eyes. The sound of her own name floated over her like soft velvet, warming and caressing her, comforting her, quieting her fears.

Yes, she thought, she could trust Slade Ironbow.

"All right," she said, tearing her gaze from his. "We'll try it. I'll be riding with you, of course."

"What?"

"This is a working ranch. Therefore, I work. I rode the range with my father from the time I was ten years old."

"You don't belong out there," Slade said, frowning.

"Oh? I suppose you feel that because I'm a woman I should sit around fluttering my eyelashes in between having babies."

"You've got something against babies?" he asked gruffly.

"Of course not, but since I don't have a husband, babies are not on my mind at the moment. I saddle up at dawn like everyone else."

Slade sat back in his chair and glared at her. "From the sound of things, I'm going to have my hands full around here as it is. I won't have time to look after you."

"No one looks after me, Slade Ironbow. I'm perfectly capable of taking care of myself. My father knew it, the men know it, and I suggest you believe it."

"When I see it," he said, his eyes narrowing, "then I'll believe it."

"Fine. If you're finished eating I'll take you to the bunkhouse. Introductions can be made tonight, and I'm sure there's a spare bed out there."

"No."

"I beg your pardon?"

"I'm staying here in the house."

Becca jumped to her feet. "You certainly are not!"

Slade stood slowly, his jaw set in a hard line as he towered over her. She stared up at him, wide-eyed.

"I'm here," he said, his voice ominously low, "not only to protect the Bonnie Blue, but you as well. That will be made clear to the men, so your lily-white reputation won't be damaged. If you insist on going out on the range, you're never to be out of my sight. In addition, you don't go into town, or off to visit with your lady friends, nothing, unless you clear it with me first. And if you ever take on riders from Four Aces all alone like you did today, I'll personally wring your pretty little neck."

She planted her hands on her hips, gulping air into her lungs before she attempted to speak.

"Slade Ironbow," she said, her voice trembling with rage, "you are—"

"Right," Maria interrupted, hurrying into the room. "Mercy me, it's so good to know you're going to be safe from harm, Becca, until this trouble with Folger is settled."

"Maria!" Becca exclaimed. "How can you take sides with this arrogant, rude man?"

"Because I love you, Becca," Maria said softly, "and because your pa loved you. Jed Colten would like knowing someone's watching over you. Now, you swallow your temper and your stubborn streak, and use the common sense the good Lord gave you. You need Slade, we all do, and you'd best get used to following his orders until Henry Folger has been stopped. Are you listening to me, Becca Colten?"

Becca glared at Maria, then Slade, then Maria again. "Yes, I'm listening," she said tightly. "We'll do this your way . . . for now, Mr. Ironbow," she added, glowering at him again. "I'll cooperate . . . for now. But I sure as hell don't have to like it." She whirled and stomped out of the room.

"Swearing again," Slade said, shaking his head. "She does have a temper."

Maria laughed. "That she does, but she said she'll cooperate, and she will. She won't smile about it, but she'll do it."

"I want the room next to hers."

"I'll make up the bed with fresh linens. Thank you, Slade, for coming. I'll rest easier tonight knowing you're here."

"Maria, do you think Jed Colten was murdered?"

"Yes, I do. Frank breaking his leg was no accident, either, in my opinion. I don't know why those horses went down, but . . ." She shook her head. "There's no proof, though."

"The town near here, Jubele, what about its sheriff? Is there any chance that he answers to Folger?"

"Brady Webster? Mercy, no. Brady's as honest as the day is long. He told me himself that Jed Colten's being thrown from his horse didn't make any sense. Brady was mighty upset when Frank was hurt the same way. But he says there's no proof of any wrongdoing."

Slade nodded.

"Well, I'll go make up your bed, Slade. I'll look in on Becca, too, and make sure she isn't still angry as a wet hen."

"She's quite a woman," Slade said, staring at the doorway Becca had disappeared through.

Maria looked at Slade, a smile curving her lips. Her smiled broadened as he continued to gaze at the doorway. When she turned to leave the room, she was humming a happy tune.

Four

Mattie slipped out of the back door of the Silver Spur and strolled across the grassy rear area. The bright moon acted like a silvery beacon to light her way, although she could have reached her destination with no difficulty on the darkest of nights.

The Silver Spur was busy but under control, the mid-week crowd low-key and relaxed. Abe knew where she went when she wanted some fresh air and a few quiet minutes, and would send someone for her if the need arose.

Mattie smiled as she saw her white swing gleaming in the moonlight, suspended by chains from the branch of a sturdy tree. Oh, how she adored her swing.

She arranged her royal-blue silk skirt around her as she sat down on the white bench. Leaning back, she set the swing in motion, then closed her eyes and took a deep breath of the spring night air.

She'd woven such fantasies on this swing, she mused.

In the five years since she'd had this private place to escape to, she'd imagined glorious things for herself, and almost all depicted her as a fine, well-bred woman. She was respected and loved, surrounded by her children and a man who cherished her.

Such hopeless dreams, Mattie thought, opening her eyes. And this night she would not be allowed the luxury of escape, for her thoughts were centered on Slade, Becca, and the Bonnie Blue. What had Slade found when he arrived at the ranch in Texas? Were Becca and Maria and Slade in great danger?

Becca and Slade. Sitting there on her swing in the peaceful glow of moonlight, Mattie would weave a splendid fantasy for them.

Becca, a bride, her shimmering gown made of yards and yards of white satin and lace, with hundreds of delicate seed pearls decorating the bodice. A gossamer veil would hide her face as she walked down the aisle to meet the man who loved her, the man she would find happiness with for all her days. Slade Ironbow.

And Slade, the groom, would be resplendent in a black suit that emphasized the night darkness of his hair and eyes, the glow of his bronzed skin. His eyes would be warm, reflecting the love in his heart for the woman who was to become his wife.

Mattie sighed. Such foolishness she was creating. Slade Ironbow would never love one woman, stay in one place. He saw himself as a creature of the wind. And Becca? Mattie really didn't know her own daughter, didn't know if she was pampered and spoiled, the product of a wealthy man who'd given his child everything she'd demanded.

And there sat Mattie Muldoon, she thought ruefully, fantasizing that Becca and Slade were perfectly suited for each other, would fall madly in love and marry with hearts bursting with joy.

Enough, she told herself. She was being silly, wanting

for Becca what she herself had always yearned for and could never have.

She sighed again and shook her head.

"That's a sad, sad sound," a voice said.

She gasped and stiffened on the swing. The moonlight clearly identified the man who stepped out of the shadows of the trees.

"Doc! You scared me. Whatever are you doing back here?"

"Looking for you." He walked over to her. "When you weren't inside, I knew there was a good chance you'd be out here on your swing."

She smiled up at him. "I didn't realize anyone knew I escaped to this spot except Abe."

"I've seen you here many times. I just stayed in the shadows, allowed you your privacy, but made sure no one bothered you. It could be dangerous out here alone with drunken cowboys on the loose." He smiled. "You always seem so content on your swing, Mattie, as though you're painting pretty pictures in your mind."

"Oh, dear, you've caught me," she said with a soft laugh. "That's exactly what I do. This is the one place where I can forget my responsibilities, everything that needs my attention and supervision, and just daydream." She pulled her skirts in and moved to one side. "Would you care to join me, Doc?"

"I'd be honored, ma'am," he said, bowing, then settled next to her on the swing. "You know, everything runs so smoothly at the Silver Spur that I doubt many people realize what an intelligent, organized businesswoman you are, Mattie. I respect that. Lord knows my record books are a scribbled mess. I've turned them over to my assistant to handle, along with the task of keeping track of what supplies we need."

"I like to be aware of everything that's going on at the Spur. I wouldn't be comfortable having anyone else doing my books or ordering goods. When I need a break from it all, I come sit on my swing."

"And a fine swing it is."

"I was so excited the day Abe hung it for me. I guess there's still a touch of a little girl hiding inside me. I sit out here and paint big beautiful pictures in my mind."

"There's nothing wrong with having dreams," Doc said. "But tonight your sigh sounded sad." He slipped one arm behind her on the top of the swing, careful not to touch her.

"Oh, sometimes I . . . Never mind. It's too beautiful a night for gloomy thoughts. Look at that sky, Doc. It's a silvery glow. Just beautiful." Her gaze swept the heavens.

Doc's eyes were riveted on her. "Just beautiful," he repeated.

Mattie glanced down at her silk skirt, smoothing wrinkles that weren't there. "I suppose I'd best get back inside."

"Not yet. I'd like to talk to you."

"Oh?" she said, still not looking at him.

"Slade's been gone for several days, but it's taken me this long to get up the courage to come here, Mattie. There are things that I want, need, to say, and I've been over it all a hundred times in my mind since Slade left. I finally decided just to speak the words, even if I do it poorly."

"Doc . . ."

"Now, just listen, Mattie Muldoon. First off, I know that you and Slade are not . . . That is, everyone thinks that the two of you are . . . Dammit, Mattie, I know you and Slade aren't lovers!"

Her head snapped up and she stared at Doc with wide eyes. "What?"

"Slade told me the truth the night before he left."

She jumped to her feet. "What!"

Doc took her hand and tugged gently. "Sit back down here."

"Slade told you that he and I . . . I swear I'll strangle that man!"

Doc laughed. "He figured as much and told me not to say anything until he was way clear of Dodge. It took me far longer than that to get up the courage, though." He tugged again on her hand. "Mattie, please, sit back down here. Please?"

She plopped back down on the swing, her eyes still wide as she stared at him. "Slade told you the truth about us? He told you that we're only friends? Slade?"

"Surprised me, too, believe me. I've never heard Slade say so much in one sitting. He said it needed saying, even though he knew you'd be ready to shoot him on sight."

"Needed saying?" Mattie repeated, nearly shouting. "Slade Ironbow has gone loco."

"No, Slade Ironbow knows that I . . . ." Doc tightened his grip on her hand. "I am deeply in love with you, Mattie Muldoon. He wanted to tell me that he wasn't standing in my way. And so, here I am, hat in hand, heart on my sleeve, telling you that I do, indeed, love you very much."

Mattie shook her head so sharply, a lock of hair escaped her chignon. "Don't say that. Doc, I'm going back inside, and we'll forget that this conversation ever took place. Just don't speak another word on the subject. Is that clear?"

"Why? Because you care nothing for me? You don't want to hurt my feelings? Why can't I say that I love you with all my heart, Mattie? I truly do, you know, and have for a long time."

"No, no," she said, shaking her head again. "You can't, and I won't hear another word of this."

"Yes, you will. I love you, and I plan to come courting. You see, Mattie, I have every intention of asking you to be my wife. I want to marry you, and have a child with you, God willing."

Pulling her hand free, Mattie leaped to her feet so quickly, the swing swayed wildly for a moment. Doc simply smiled at her.

"You're the one who's loco," she declared, then narrowed her eyes. "Have you been drinking?"

"Not a drop."

She planted her hands on her hips. "I won't listen to this for another minute. This isn't kind, Doctor Willis. Not kind at all. If this is your idea of a joke, I find no humor in it."

He rose to stand in front of her. "It's the truth. I love you."

"You can't! Doc, I'm Mattie Muldoon, the owner of the Silver Spur saloon. Remember?"

"Best saloon in Dodge City."

"I made my living early on as one of the girls, Doc, and you know that."

"That was a long time ago. We all have things in our past best forgotten."

"Forgotten?" she repeated, her voice rising. "No one has forgotten, including me. Besides, everyone believes I've been Slade's woman all these years."

"But I know differently, and I'm the one who's in love with you."

"You are not in love with me!"

He took a step closer to her and cradled her face in his hands. "Oh, but I am."

Run! Mattie's mind screamed. He was going to kiss her, she could tell, and she mustn't allow this to happen. But how many nights had she sat on her swing, dreaming of Doc Willis kissing her, holding her . . . No! Run!

"I'm going to kiss you now, Mattie," he said huskily.

No! "Yes," she whispered. "No, no, I—"

He lowered his head and claimed her mouth in a kiss

so soft, so sweet, that tears sprang to Mattie's eyes. Her knees trembled, and she clutched his shoulders for support. The kiss intensified as he dropped his hands to her back and pulled her to him, crushing her breasts against his chest.

Oh, yes, Mattie thought dreamily. She'd waited for this, imagined this. Doc was there, at last. He was kissing her, holding her, igniting within her a desire she'd thought long dead.

He slowly lifted his head, but didn't release her as he gazed into her eyes. "I love you, Mattie. I want to marry you and spend the rest of my life with you. Maybe you'll never come to love me as I love you, but if you care for me even a little, I'll count myself the luckiest man. It'll be the happiest, proudest day of my life when you become my wife."

Mattie fell from her hazy fantasies with a painful thud. "Proud? Oh, Doc, you're insane. I was a whore. I run a house of pleasure. There's nothing about me to make any man proud. I'm alone, I always will be, and I take care of myself. You'd be proud to have me as your wife? You have truly lost all sense. I accepted my life as it is years ago. You best accept it, too, and stop this foolishness this very instant."

Doc gently gripped her shoulders and gave her a small shake. "I won't hear another word of your saying I shouldn't be proud to call you my wife. I'm coming courting, Miss Muldoon. Get used to that idea, because the whole town is going to know quite well what I'm doing."

"Oh, dear Lord," she whispered. "Doc, would you think clearly for one second? Everyone in Dodge believes that Slade and I . . . They'll be waiting for Slade to come back and call you out and . . ."

"These folks will just have to live with the disappointment that Slade Ironbow isn't going to shoot me dead," Doc said dryly.

"Well, I'm going to shoot *him* dead!" she exclaimed. "This is so wrong. You're a respectable citizen of Dodge City and I'm a—"

"Don't say it," Doc warned her. "You're speaking of the woman I love and intend to marry." He paused and smiled at her. "I'll bid you good night now, Miss Muldoon."

"But—"

He pulled her close and gave her a hard, fast kiss. She staggered when he released her.

"Good night, ma'am," he said formally. "It has indeed been a pleasure speaking with you, and sharing your swing. Oh, and my name is Jim. From here on out, you'll call me Jim." He strode past her and left.

She spun around and watched him go. "But, Doc . . ."

"Jim," he repeated over his shoulder. "I'll come calling tomorrow, Miss Muldoon."

As he disappeared into the darkness, Mattie sank onto the swing and stared after him. Her fingertips came to rest on her lips, and she relived the feel and taste of Doc's mouth on hers.

"I never knew his name was Jim," she whispered.

At noon the next day, Dr. James Willis entered the general store owned and operated by the Widow Sullivan. While there were two other general stores in Dodge, one larger and better stocked than this one, Doc had made his choice carefully. This store had exactly what he needed—Widow Sullivan, and her reputation for being the busiest gossip in all of Dodge City. If you did it, Widow Sullivan knew about it. And she had perfected her ability to spread any news, large or small, interesting or dull, as fast as a greased pig.

"Good day, Widow Sullivan," Doc said as he strode into the store, touching his fingertips to the brim of his hat.

He walked directly to the counter and delivered his very best smile to the tall, broad woman standing behind it.

"Howdy do, Doc," the widow said in her booming voice. "What can I do for you today?"

Doc sighed dramatically. "I find myself in a great dilemma, ma'am."

"Is that a fact?" Widow Sullivan asked, leaning toward him, eyes sparkling with anticipation. "Well, why don't you just tell me all your troubles. It's truly amazing how much help can come from an extra mind working on a problem."

"Well, you see, I'm going courting and—"

Widow Sullivan clasped her hands together in delight. "You're going courting? Land's sake, this is marvelous, just marvelous. It's time you had yourself a wife, Doc Willis, if I do say so myself."

"My sentiments exactly," he said, nodding. "My problem is I don't know where to start. I'm going calling today, and feel I should take a small token to my lady. But"—he threw up his hands in despair—"I have no idea what would be proper."

"I have the perfect thing," Widow Sullivan gushed. "Came from back East. Chocolates in a pretty box. Most highfalutin thing I ever saw."

"Are you sure it's proper to take chocolates to a lady the first time I go calling?"

"Mercy, yes. And you say, 'Sweets for the sweet.' "

Doc groaned silently. "Yes, ma'am, I'll surely remember to say that."

"Wonderful." The widow removed a small, gold-foil box from a shelf behind the counter and placed it in front of Doc. "That's fifty cents."

Doc paid her and picked up the box. "Thank you for all your help. You're really most kind." He turned to leave. "Good day."

"Oh, Doc?" the widow called, smiling brightly.

He looked back at her. "Yes?"

"I'm just a lonely widow, you know, and the news of love simply warms my heart. It would bring such sunshine into my life if you'd share the name of the dear woman you're courting."

Doc opened his mouth to answer just as the door opened and two women, Emma Virginia Tappitt and her daughter, entered the store. He slid them a quick look, then raised his voice when he spoke.

"It would brighten your day to know who I'm courting, Widow Sullivan?" he asked. "Who I'm going calling on to give these chocolates to?"

"Oh, my, yes," Widow Sullivan said.

Emma Virginia and her daughter inched closer.

"I see no harm in telling you who it is," Doc said, "since my intentions are strictly honorable. I intend to make her my wife, if she'll have me. I have to convince her that I'm good husband material."

"Nonsense," Emma Virginia said. "You're the best catch in town, Doc Willis. Unless she's a silly fool, she'll know that."

"Doc was speaking to me, Emma Virginia," Widow Sullivan said huffily. "Go on, Doc."

"Yes," he said. "The object of my affections, my bright star, my one and only is . . ."

"Yes, yes?" Widow Sullivan said.

"Miss Mattie Muldoon." He beamed. "Good day to you, ladies."

With that, Dr. Jim Willis went out of the store, leaving three shocked women staring after him with their mouths open and their eyes wide.

Doc strode along the wooden sidewalk, nodding at men and smiling and touching the brim of his hat as he passed women. The box of chocolates was tucked securely under his arm.

When he reached the Silver Spur, he saw that the

double doors behind the louvered half-doors were closed. He knocked briskly, and a minute later Abe opened one of the doors.

"Howdy, Doc," he said. "Thought you knew we don't open until the middle of the afternoon."

"I've come to see Mattie."

"Oh, well, that's fine, I guess. They're all just sitting here drinking coffee. If you don't mind seeing a bunch of women in their dressing gowns and no paint on their faces, come on in."

"Thank you, Abe."

Doc squared his shoulders and entered the saloon. Mattie and her girls were sitting around two tables. It was odd to see the Spur empty of men, and the girls looking no different from Dodge's most respected matrons, first thing in the morning. Mattie sat up straight when she saw him, and all of the women turned to stare at him.

"Good day, ladies," he said.

"Doc," Mattie whispered, rising slowly. She was wearing a green silk dressing gown and her hair was loose, tumbling in waves past her shoulders.

"Jim," he said, striding confidently toward her. "You're to call me Jim, remember?" He extended the box of chocolates to her, and she took it into her shaking hands. "These are for you. I have officially begun my courting of you, Miss Muldoon, just as I said I would." He leaned down and brushed his lips over hers. "Widow Sullivan said I was to say 'Sweets for the sweet' when I gave you the chocolates. So, consider it said."

"Widow Sullivan knows that . . ." Mattie gasped. "Oh, Doc, what have you done?"

"Started courting you, ma'am." He smiled and tipped his hat, then spun on his heel and left the saloon.

Mattie stared at the door, the box of chocolates, then the door again. "Oh, dear Lord."

Abe shook his head. "There's trouble ahead, there's bad trouble ahead. When Slade Ironbow hears of this . . . Oh, there is trouble ahead."

"Abe, hush," Mattie said, sinking back onto her chair.

Ellen, one of the girls, sighed dreamily. "A real gentleman comin' a courtin'. That is just the finest thing I ever did see."

"You best see it real fast," Abe said. "Doc Willis will be in his grave when Slade gets back."

"Stop it, Abe," Mattie said, running a fingertip over the gold-foil box.

"You know Slade's going to shoot Doc dead," Abe said. "Too bad. I like Doc. Him and Slade is friends too. Slade will have to shoot him, though. Call him out, of course, to keep it legal."

"Maybe Slade won't hear tell of this," Belle said.

"Didn't you listen to Doc?" Abe asked. "The Widow Sullivan knows."

"Oh." Belle shrugged. "That settles that. All of Dodge City knows."

"Yep," Abe said. "I'm going to miss Doc. Thought he had more brains than this. He just signed his own death papers."

"Abraham, that is enough," Mattie said sternly. "This is the first box of chocolates I've ever received in my life; now don't you go and ruin it for me. I will, somehow, get Doc Willis to stop this nonsense of his, but at the moment I'd like to enjoy my chocolates."

Abe grinned. "Yes, ma'am. Must admit that's a right fancy box he brought you."

"Could you open it?" Ellen asked. "We wouldn't dream of askin' you for none, but I never saw chocolates before. Did Doc say his name was Jim?"

"Yes," Mattie said, carefully lifting the cover of the box. "Jim."

"Fancy that," Belle said. "I thought his name was Doc.

JOAN ELLIOTT PICKART

Oh, look! Oh, Mattie, aren't they beautiful? So that's chocolates. See how they're sittin' in a paper basket, each and every one? Amazing. They smell funny, but they sure are pretty."

All the girls gathered around Mattie, peering into the box and oohing and aahing over the treasure.

Mattie blinked back her tears as she stared at the chocolates. Oh, Jim, she thought dismally. Dumb, darling Jim. What a fool thing to have gone and done. The news that Doc Willis was courting Mattie Muldoon would be all over Dodge by nightfall, thanks to Widow Sullivan. Doc had stirred up a hornet's nest, and Mattie had no idea how to quiet it. He would be hurt by his actions, his reputation soiled by his courting her. She'd told Abe she'd stop Doc somehow, but what if it was too late, the damage already done?

"Well," she said, forcing a lightness to her voice, "I must be getting upstairs." She put the lid back on the chocolates and stood up. "I have to work on the books." Carrying the golden box, she hurried across the room and up the stairs.

"Was she crying?" Bella asked, frowning.

"I would be if someone came courtin' and brought me chocolates," Ellen said. "Sure never goin' to happen to me. Imagine a real gentleman comin' courtin'."

"A dead gentleman," Abe said.

"Abe," Belle said, "shut up."

"Maybe Slade is ready for a change of women," Clara said, fluffing her hair. "He does take a fancy to me at times, you know."

"Clara," Belle said, "shut up." Clara slouched back in her chair and pouted. "Those chocolates sure were pretty," Belle went on, "but didn't you think they smelled funny?"

"Belle," two women said in unison, "shut up."

• • •

56

Upstairs, Mattie restlessly paced her sitting room, her gaze continually drawn to the shiny, gold-foil box of chocolates sitting on one of the tables. She hadn't slept well the night before, and had awakened feeling as tired as when she'd gone to bed. Now, her head was pounding as she replayed in her mind the scene with Doc downstairs. How could he have done such a fool thing, bought chocolates from Widow Sullivan, then marched right up to the Spur in broad daylight?

Mattie walked into the bedroom and brushed back the curtain over the window. Below, her swing gleamed in the sun and swayed slightly in the breeze. Memories of the previous night rushed over her—memories of being held in Jim's arms, being kissed by him, hearing him say that he loved her and wanted her to be his wife. A magical night, best forgotten. A night she knew she would never forget.

A now-familiar ache tightened her throat, and she had neither the strength nor the desire to stop the tears that filled her eyes. She was going to cry. She was going to cry because she was tired, her head hurt, and she was worried about Becca, and Slade, and Doc. She was going to cry because at the moment she didn't know how to solve her problems. She was going to cry because she was alone and lonely.

And when she was finished crying, she decided, as the tears started to fall, she would figure out what she was going to do.

"Hey, Doc. Can I talk to you for a minute?"

Doc looked up from his desk at the small man standing in his office doorway. Dressed in a black suit, the man was nervously twirling his hat in his hands.

"Howdy, Harvey," Doc said. "How's the funeral business?"

"Fair."

"What can I do for you? I really don't have any bodies lying around here waiting for your services."

"No, no, of course you don't. I . . . um . . . Well, Doc, a man needs to be looking ahead in his life, making plans for . . . things."

"Things?" Doc repeated, raising his eyebrows.

"Yes. You see, if you pay in advance for your coffin and burial, you don't add financial burden to your grieving kin. Yes, sir, a man needs to look ahead. I've got a special price for you, Doc, that you can't afford to pass up. Think of the peace of mind it will give you to know this is all tended to."

"I'm not planning on dying in the near future, Harvey," Doc said pleasantly, "but thanks for dropping by and making me an offer."

"You're not being considerate of your kin," Harvey said. "They'll be stuck with your burial costs when Mr. Iron-bow—that is . . . Well, I'll be seeing you, Doc." He spun around and started back through the door.

"Hold it!"

Harvey stopped and turned tentatively to face him again. "Yes?"

"Are you saying you came here to give me a cut rate for my funeral now, because you figure I'll be dead once Slade Ironbow gets back here?"

"Oh, well, I . . ."

"Harvey?"

"Hell's fire, Doc, the word is out that you're courting Mattie Muldoon. Now I'm not one to pass judgment. By the time I deal with folks, they're in no position to be expressing their opinion on anything. But facts are facts, Doc, and as a businessman I have to be practical. It would be a kindness to your kin to pay for your funeral now, because everyone knows your days are numbered.

Slade Ironbow is going to shoot you into tomorrow when he finds out you been courting Mattie Muldoon."

Dr. James Willis put his head back and roared with laughter. Harvey inched his way out the door, his eyes wide with shock. He told the next six people he saw that Doc Willis was not in his right mind.

When Doc's assistant entered the office twenty minutes later, he found his mentor trying to cure himself of a painful case of the hiccups.

Five

Slade was up before dawn. As he strode to the kitchen, he knew that the scowl he'd seen on his face while he'd shaved was still firmly in place. He had not slept well, tossing and turning throughout the night, his bed linens ending up on the floor in a tangled heap.

Always before he'd slept when he commanded his body to do so. He'd perfected the knack of grabbing quick naps and awakening refreshed. When he slept, he did so lightly, a section of his mind alert for any hint of danger. But not last night. He couldn't remember ever being so consumed by thoughts that he'd been unable to relax and sleep.

Consumed by thoughts of Becca Colten.

Hearing her moving around in the room next to his, he'd been able to see her in his mind's eye so clearly, she might as well have been in *his* room. He'd remembered how anger had flashed in her eyes; how her prim, high-necked mourning dress had molded to her full breasts and her waist, so tiny he was sure he could circle it with his hands. He'd pictured her brushing her hair until it shone like an auburn waterfall tumbling down her back.

Oh, yes, he thought dryly, stopping outside the kitchen door, he'd spent a very long, uncomfortable night, thanks to Miss Colten. His wandering mind had lingered on the tantalizing shape of her lips, and he'd envisioned himself taking Becca into his arms and covering her mouth with his. His body had grown hard, aching with desire, as he'd imagined lowering her to the bed and meshing his body with hers.

Nothing like this had ever happened to him before!

"Damn," he muttered, then pushed open the door and strode heavily into the kitchen.

Maria was standing in front of the stove, and glanced up when she heard him. " 'Morning, Slade. Coffee is ready and the eggs will be along in a few minutes. Sun's coming up. Shouldn't be too hot out on the range this time of year. Another month, though, and we'll be feeling the heat."

Slade poured coffee into a mug, then sat at the wooden table.

"Hope you don't mind eating breakfast in the kitchen," Maria went on. "Becca and Jed always took their breakfast out here."

"Fine," he said.

He took off his Stetson and set it on the chair next to him. So, where was Miss Colten? he wondered. Still in bed, probably. She'd no doubt slept like a baby and would get up when she was good and ready. For all her talk about riding with him, he was sure it was at her leisure, whenever the mood struck. She'd be in no hurry to leave the comforts of her fancy house with Maria waiting on her hand and foot.

The back door opened and Becca strode in. "Slade," she said coolly, nodding at him as she headed for the coffeepot on the stove.

Slade's gaze skimmed over her body. She was clad in dark denim pants that emphasized the slimness of her hips and length of her legs. She wore boots and a white cotton shirt, and her hair was plaited into a single braid that hung down her back.

She poured her coffee and started toward the table. He watched her with heavy-lidded eyes, unable to look away from her breasts, barely discernible beneath the shirt. When she sat down opposite him, his gaze lifted to the lips that had helped create his unsettled night. He felt his body tighten, and his anger increased.

"I was out to the bunkhouse," she said, not looking at him. "I wanted to make sure the men didn't leave until they'd met you. I told them your name, said you were the new foreman until Frank's leg is healed, and that you were also my bodyguard of sorts, which was why you were staying in the house."

She paused and sipped her coffee. When Slade didn't comment, she continued.

"Some of the men have heard of you. They were buzzing among themselves when I left. They'll wait until you speak to them before they head out to start their chores."

"Hot food," Maria said, bustling across the large room with two plates. "Eggs, bacon, hash browns. Now, you dig in and clean those plates, both of you."

"Thank you," Becca said, smiling at her.

"Thanks," Slade said gruffly.

"Do you always wake up this cheerfully, Mr. Ironbow," Becca asked sweetly, "or is this a special treat for the Bonnie Blue?"

"Becca," Maria said warningly as she returned to the stove, "mind your manners."

Slade scooped up some eggs, then glanced at Becca. "Do you always go around dressed like a man?"

She stiffened. "I beg your pardon?"

"You heard me," he said, munching on a crisp slice of bacon.

"These are my working clothes, Mr. Ironbow, and are quite appropriate for a working ranch."

"And appropriate for wiggling your cute little behind in front of a bunch of randy cowboys," he said tightly. "A lady doesn't wear pants!"

"Wiggling my . . ." Becca sputtered. "You are despicable, Mr. Ironbow."

"Slade.'"

"Dammit, you're infuriating!"

He lifted one shoulder in a shrug. "A lady doesn't swear, either, so I suppose the pants are, as you say, appropriate. Eat your breakfast." He redirected his attention to his plate.

"Now, you listen to me," Becca said, leaning toward him. "You have no right to make comments about what I wear when I—"

"What happened to the horses your father and Frank were riding when they went down?" he asked, interrupting her.

She blinked. "What?"

"The horses. Where are they?"

Becca sat back in her chair. "My father's horse broke its leg and had to be destroyed. Frank's is in the barn."

Slade nodded and continued to eat.

"Why?" she asked. "Why do you want to know about the horses?"

"I intend to look at Frank's," Slade said. "Eat up or go hungry. I want to get started."

She glared at him and picked up her fork. The remainder of the meal passed in strained silence. Slade cleaned his plate, put on his Stetson, and stood.

"Let's go," he said.

Becca's gaze slid over him as she drained her coffee cup. Damn the man, she thought. There he stood, towering above her, barking orders like he owned the place . . . and looking so ruggedly handsome, that strange heat throbbed deep within her again. Standing so close to her, so tall, strong, dark, he made her remember the shocking, wanton dreams she'd had the night before. Dreams in which he'd embraced her, kissed her, then reached for the buttons of her dress . . .

"I'm ready," she said, jumping to her feet as she felt her cheeks flush. She strode to the back door. "Thank you for breakfast, Maria," she said as she lifted a white Stetson from a peg by the door. Then she left.

"Slade," Maria said.

"Yes?" He turned to look at her.

"Go easy on her."

"She doesn't belong out there."

"She always rode with her pa."

"There's trouble now."

"She's a Colten, and that means she doesn't run from trouble. She's grieving for her pa, but she won't let you see her tears. Becca is strong in some ways, but needs caring for in others. Try to be patient with her, Slade. She needs you here, but she doesn't want to admit how frightened she is of Folger and what he might do. Surely you can understand pride."

Slade looked at Maria for a long moment, then turned and left the house without a further word.

More than thirty men were gathered outside the barn. Slade could see Becca talking to a short, wiry man, who appeared to be in his fifties. As Slade approached a silence fell over the group. All eyes were riveted on him when he stopped in front of them.

He pushed his Stetson back and studied each man's face, one at a time. Tension hung heavily in the air.

Some men met Slade's scrutiny head-on; others couldn't hold his gaze and stared down at the ground.

"You know who I am," he said finally. "I'm not one for speeches, so listen good. I'm in charge. When I give orders I expect them to be followed, no questions asked. Folger will be stopped . . . my way. The Bonnie Blue and Miss Colten will be protected . . . my way "

He looked at Becca. She opened her mouth as though to speak, then snapped it closed.

"If you have a gun and holster," he went on, "wear it. Check your rifle in the boot of your saddle every morning. Pair up. No man rides alone. If a steer gets away, let it go if your partner isn't free to go after it with you. Cover your backs. Stay alert. If you're mending fences, work one on each side. Fire two shots if you see any sign of trouble, anything that doesn't look right to you. When any of us hear those two shots, we'll drop what we're doing and come. If you don't like what I'm saying, pack your gear and clear out now."

He stopped speaking and tugged his Stetson low again, shadowing his eyes. No one spoke. A few men restlessly shifted their feet; someone cleared his throat. Slade waited. The short man Becca had been talking to stepped forward, and all eyes were trained on him.

"Name's Yancey Perkins, Mr. Ironbow," he said, extending his hand. "I'm mighty glad you're here to take over. These here are a good bunch of boys. They'll follow your orders, or I'll pay 'em off and send 'em on their way. What I'm sayin' is, count me in."

Slade shook Yancey's hand. "Slade will do."

Yancey turned to the men. "So? If you're leaving, do it now. Don't stand around on Bonnie Blue land breathing in Bonnie Blue air unless you're willin' to fight to keep it out of Folger's hands."

"Hell, Yancey," someone said, "the Bonnie Blue is home to most of us. We're not goin' nowhere. Pete here will be my partner on the range. I'll stick so close, you'll think I'm in love with him. Mr. Ironbow . . . um, Slade, I'm in."

Slade nodded.

"And you drifters?" Yancey asked. "Some of you ain't been here long. You goin' or stayin'?"

"I'm staying," a young man said. "I came all the way from Pennsylvania to work on this ranch. That polecat Folger isn't driving me off. I've heard of you, Slade. Word is you're about as fast as they come with that gun, and you've never drawn first on a man. Also heard you do some special work for the President when he asks you."

Becca's gaze flew to Slade, but with the hat shading his face, she couldn't read his expression.

"Well, I don't suppose," the young cowboy went on, "you can talk about special and secret doings for the President and all. Anyway, I'm in. You're honest, I hear tell, and that's all adding up to good enough for me."

"I've been told he's a bounty hunter," Becca heard someone say quietly.

"Naw," the man beside him said in a louder voice. "He's hired private by folks wantin' somebody called out for a fair draw."

Her eyes wide, Becca turned as Bob Smith, a cowboy who'd been at the Bonnie Blue for five years, spat tobacco on the ground.

"Well," he said to the three men around him, "he's fast with that gun, and we need help dealing with Folger. I'm countin' myself lucky that Slade showed up here."

Other men added their agreement. No one started toward the bunkhouse to pack his gear.

"Good bunch of boys," Yancey said to Slade, grinning.

"Thank you," Becca said to the men. "Thank you all very much."

"Your pa was a fine man, Miss Colten," Bob Smith said. "We'll settle this with Folger, don't you worry none."

"Damn straight," Bucky said, puffing out his chest.

Someone whopped him on the back, and he nearly toppled over.

"Yancey," Slade asked, "what work was scheduled for today?"

"Half the men mending fences, half moving a bunch of steers from the south end up over to the north ridge to graze."

"Saddle up, then," Slade ordered. "Pair off. If the number is uneven, do three. No one is alone. Miss Colten goes with me."

Talking among themselves, the men ambled into the barn to saddle their horses, some tipping their hats to Becca as they passed her. She watched them go, then walked over to Slade.

"That went very well," she said, smiling up at him. "I'm pleased. My father would be pleased, too, to know they were all loyal to the Bonnie Blue."

Slade looked down at her, and felt his heart instantly beat faster. Lord, she was beautiful. It was the first time he'd seen her smile like that. Her eyes were warm, and those lips . . . Damn, it was sweet torture just to look at Becca's lips. To imagine kissing them . . .

Becca's smile faded, replaced by a frown. She cocked her head to one side as she studied Slade's scowl.

"Why are you so angry?" she asked. "Everything went just fine with the men. They'll follow your orders, I'm sure of that."

"I want to speak with Frank," he said, ignoring her question.

She sighed. "All right. He's in the bunkhouse."

She started toward the low, long building. Slade waited for a moment, then caught up with her. They walked in silence as the men came out of the barn and trotted by on their horses. When the last man had disappeared in a cloud of dust, Slade glanced down at Becca.

"They're loyal to the Colten name," he said, "not just the Bonnie Blue."

She looked up at him in surprise. "What a nice thing to say."

He chuckled. "I'm a nice person once or twice a year."

Heaven help her, Becca thought, nearly forgetting to breathe. Slade's smile softened his stern, rugged features, and even warmed the cold depths of his eyes.

"You have a marvelous smile," she said, hoping her voice was steady. "You should use it more often."

He shrugged. She pulled her gaze from his and reached for the handle to the bunkhouse door. Slade moved at the same moment, and his hand closed over hers.

Heat from his hand seemed to envelop Becca, and she again forgot to breathe. There was such strength in his big hand, she thought, staring at it, and such gentleness, too.

Her hand was so small, Slade thought, seeing it disappear beneath his. And fragile and soft. He'd have to be careful with her, very gentle as he peeled away her clothes—

He jerked his hand away with a smothered curse. "Open the door," he said gruffly.

Becca yanked on it. "You change moods so fast, no one could begin to keep up."

"Don't try."

"I don't intend to." She shot him a cool look, then stalked into the building.

The large bunkhouse was divided into two sections, one for sleeping, one for eating. Wooden tables were lined in rows, and two men were cleaning away the debris from breakfast. Becca smiled at them, then turned to the left and crossed the room.

"Frank?" she called outside a closed door. "It's Becca. May I come in?"

"You bet," a voice answered.

She opened the door and entered the sleeping area,

with Slade right behind her. The room was neat, each bunk made up. Against one wall were round tables for playing cards, and several worn but comfortable chairs sat by a small bookcase containing several much-read books and newspapers. Frank's bed was the nearest to the door. As foreman of the ranch, he had a partition that afforded him some privacy.

"Hello, Frank," Becca said, stopping at the foot of the bed. "How's the leg?"

"Giving me fits." Frank shifted his gaze to Slade. "Howdy, Slade. Damn glad to hear you're taking charge around here."

Slade narrowed his eyes as Becca glanced quickly between the two men.

"You know Slade?" she asked Frank.

"Yep," he said. "I can tell he doesn't remember me, though."

Frank who? Slade wondered, searching his mind. About forty, the foreman was well-built and good-looking, with curly brown hair. Frank. Frankie . . .

"Frankie Tatum," he said, grinning. "Seven, eight years ago, San Antonio."

"You saved my swaggering hide, Slade." He turned to Becca to explain. "I was taking a little side trip after a cattle drive from the Bonnie Blue. I was so drunk I couldn't see, and very convinced that a darlin' saloon gal was in love with me. Never mind that she belonged to Digger McHugh, I was going to have her, by damn."

Slade nodded. "Digger took exception to your choice of women."

"Exception?" Frank said, with a hoot of laughter. Then he groaned and clutched his leg. "Digger was going to shoot me into the next county."

"How lovely," Becca said dryly.

"Slade here stepped in, Miss Colten, even though he didn't know me from Adam. Never saw anyone draw so fast as Slade. He just talked real low, told Digger he was taking me out of there and nobody was going to get hurt. I passed out about then. One of the other men from the Bonnie Blue told me Slade hoisted me over his shoulder while he kept his gun on Digger. He dumped me in a horse trough, I came to, and we rode like blazes out of town. What a night. We made camp and come morning Slade was gone, and I had a headache that I thought would split my head right open. Never did thank you for saving my hide, Slade, so I'm doing it now. Never knew why you bothered, either."

"Digger and I didn't get along very well," Slade said. "I couldn't see letting him kill a man who was too drunk to know his own mind." Slade nodded at Frank's splinted leg. "I see you're still getting into trouble."

"I'm mad as hell about this," Frank said. "Can't figure out why my horse went down. Shouldn't have happened, any more than Jed Colten being thrown. Sorry, Miss Colten, I don't mean to upset you by speaking of your pa."

"That's all right," she said softly. "I'll never believe my father's death was an accident. Your breaking your leg wasn't an accident, either, but there's no proof to the contrary."

"Yet," Slade said.

"Meaning?" Frank asked.

"We'll see. Tell me about Folger."

"He's scum. He was afraid of Jed Colten, but the day of Jed's funeral, Folger got drunk and told anyone who would listen that he was going to make the Bonnie Blue his, that it needed a man to run it. He's thirty-five or six, but soft. Got a drinking belly and doesn't do a lick of work at Four Aces. He hires anyone who's good with a gun. Folger's pa built Four Aces up into a fine spread, but he died of a heart attack two years ago. Henry Folger is letting the ranch slide. He doesn't get a good day's work out of hired guns, but he's hell-bent on having the Bonnie Blue. He's drinking more and more, I hear. He's a dangerous man, Slade, but even drunk he's smart. The sheriff can't pin a thing on him. Folger took care of Jed and me, and there's no telling what he might do next. Damn, I'm mighty glad you're here. Does Folger know?"

"He knows."

"Then watch your back."

"Always do." Slade walked over to a few other bunks and returned with three pillows. Without speaking he carefully lifted Frank's broken leg and positioned the pillows beneath it. "Try that. I'll check in with you later."

"Thanks," Frank said. "Everything is going to be fine, Miss Colten. Slade, if any of the boys give you trouble, send them to me. I'll set them straight about following your orders."

"I don't think there's going to be any problem with the men," Becca said.

Frank looked at Slade for a long moment. "No, I doubt there will be."

"Try to rest, Frank," Becca said, then smiled. "Or is it Frankie?"

"Don't know why I called myself Frankie that night in San Antonio. Fact is, I don't know why I did half of what I did."

"Boys will be boys," Becca said, heading for the door. " 'Bye, Frankie."

"Good day to you, too, Miss Colten," Frank said, smiling.

Slade watched Becca go, then turned back to Frank. "I don't want her out on the range. I've got enough to do without watching over her too."

"She always went out with her pa. Besides, she's better off out there with you than left unprotected in the house. Folger won't bother Maria, I don't figure, but I'd hate to think about Becca being alone with no one but Maria with her."

"You've got a point."

"Folger's a snake in the grass, Slade. Be very careful."

Slade nodded and left the bunkhouse. He found Becca waiting for him outside.

"I want to see Frank's horse," he said.

She nodded. "Small world, isn't it?" she said as they started toward the barn. "You saved Frank's life years ago, and now you meet up with each other again. That was a wonderful thing you did that night in San Antonio."

"I didn't like Digger."

"You saved a man's life. And you're here as a favor to someone else, not because you personally owed my father a debt. You're a very complicated man."

Slade didn't comment.

"Do you really work for the President?"

Slade still didn't comment.

Becca threw up her hands in exasperation. "Is the weather a safe topic? Nice day, isn't it?"

"Yep," he said, a smile tugging at his lips.

She glared at him.

The barn was huge and neat as a pin. There was a place for everything, and everything was obviously in its place. The sweet smell of hay mingled with the aroma of horses, and Slade inhaled the fragrance.

"Frank's horse is in the third stall there," Becca said, pointing

Slade stroked the horse's nose before opening the half-door and entering the stall. He hunkered down, balancing his weight on the balls of his feet, and spoke in a low, steady voice to the animal.

Becca watched the jittery horse calm within moments, and realized that she, too, was nearly mesmerized by the soothing sound of Slade's voice.

Her gaze swept over him, lingering on his strong back, the muscles rippling beneath his shirt as he examined the horse's front legs. Then her gaze lowered to his hard thighs, which his denims molded to perfectly. Heat suffused her, and she quickly looked at his hands instead. He was gently probing the horse's legs. She remembered the feel of his hand closing over hers on the bunkhouse door, remembered its strength, and the heat within her soared.

Slade was magnificent, she thought. In the few hours he'd been at the Bonnie Blue, she felt changed. Her senses had heightened, and everything around her was clearer, sharper, more vivid. Anticipation was building within her, as though Slade was going to reveal some mystery to her. No other man had ever aroused such sensations in her, and she wondered where it would lead . . . with Slade.

"Damn," he said, pushing himself to his feet. His jaw was set in a hard line as he stepped out of the stall and closed the door. "Becca," he asked, stroking the horse's neck, "do you know where Frank went down?"

"Yes."

"Let's saddle up and get out there. I want to have a look around."

She stared at Frank's horse, as though hoping it would tell her what was going on in Slade's mind, then hurried to saddle her own mount.

Six

The morning air was comfortably cool, the sky a brilliant blue. Slade Ironbow riding a horse, Becca decided, was a glorious sight to behold. They moved as one, man and animal, in a graceful flow of beautifully synchronized power.

"Why didn't you name your horse?" she asked after they'd been riding about half an hour. Her own horse was a dappled gray she'd named Misty.

"Why did you name yours?" he countered, glancing at her.

"Well, because . . . she's mine."

"My horse belongs to himself and the wind. He'll stay with me for as long as *he* chooses. Not all Indians believe that, but my father does, and he taught it to me. My mother always named her horses, and my father said that was fine."

"Your mother is a white woman?"

"Was. She died when I was twelve."

"Then you understand the pain of losing a parent, someone you loved dearly."

"Not really," he said dispassionately. "I didn't know my mother very well." He paused. "This is beautiful land on the Bonnie Blue. In fact, it's one of the finest spreads I've seen."

"Thank you," she said absently. Why wouldn't a twelve-year-old boy have known his mother well? she wondered. Where had she been if not with her husband and son? Slade obviously didn't wish to talk about it, and she knew better than to press. All she'd get would be his infuriating silence or one-word answers.

He suddenly reined in his horse, snapping Becca back to attention. She stopped next to him and waited for him to speak.

"Look," he said, gazing off into the distance. "There are miles of wildflowers sweeping up over that rise. I've seen patterned rugs back East, imported from countries like Persia and Turkey, that are symbols of wealth and high social status. But I'd rather have a carpet of wildflowers like that." He took a deep breath. "That's nature's perfume. Nothing is more beautiful."

Becca stared at him intently, a smile slowly curving her lips. Not many men, she mused, shifting her gaze to the rolling fields of vibrant flowers, would stop to look at wildflowers. Slade obviously loved the land and the gifts of nature that came from it. It would take a man such as him to understand her devotion to the Bonnie Blue.

Slade nudged his horse forward, once again pulling Becca from her reverie. A gust of wind swept over them, stirring the dust in its path.

She laughed. "The wind brought a different perfume. The odor of cattle. Personally, I find it heady and rich, but I doubt the people you know in the East would be impressed."

"No, I don't think they would. Becca, did Jed give you a

chance to enjoy the things young girls do, or did he treat you more like a son, bring you out here on the range with him whether you wanted to be here or not?"

"Oh, no, it wasn't like that at all. I pestered him until he gave up and allowed me to ride with him. He insisted I go to school in town and spend time with Maria learning my manners and social graces, but I was always happiest when I was turned loose to ride on the Bonnie Blue.

"I know people are saying I'm destined to be a spinster, especially now that I sent Henry Folger packing. All of my friends are married with a baby or two, but . . ." She shrugged. "I'd like to have a family, but it would be a rare man who would understand and tolerate my love of this land."

Slade nodded. *He* understood. "I move between two worlds: the Indian's and the white man's. I prefer the way of life of my father's people, living off the land. I don't like being in the city for too long at a time. I feel stifled, closed in."

"Yes," Becca said. Slade understood.

They rode in silence for several minutes, the breeze bringing the various scents of flowers and cattle, the musky odor of water holes. Cows bellowed in the distance, adding their voices to the sound of plodding horses' hooves, the buzzing of bees, the occasional shriek of a hawk soaring across the clear blue sky. The sun rose higher in the heavens, adding its warmth to the peaceful scene.

"How did you do with spring calves?" Slade asked, breaking the comfortable silence that had fallen between them.

"Very well. A record number were born, and they're all branded. They'll be ready for the midsummer cattle drive to Houston. My father put his foot down on that, and I was never allowed to go on the cattle drives. Now? We'll see."

"Who handles the paperwork, the records for the ranch?"

She wrinkled her nose. "I do, and it's not my favorite chore, believe me. It keeps me cooped up inside far too long." She paused. "There, up ahead. Frank went down in that wide gap between those two sets of rocks."

When they reached the spot Slade pulled up and swung out of his saddle. He dropped the horse's reins to the ground as Becca tied hers to a mesquite tree.

She looked at his horse. "He won't wander?"

"Not unless he wants to. He's never wanted to."

"One of these days, Mr. Ironbow, you're liable to have a very long walk facing you if that horse has a change of heart."

"Yep." He hunkered down and brushed aside the short, stiff scrub and bunchgrass that grew around the rocks.

"What are you looking for?" she asked.

"What I figure to find."

"In other words, you'll tell me when you're ready to."

"Yep."

Ten minutes passed, then twenty, as Slade went over the area, practically one blade of grass at a time. At last he straightened and climbed the ten-foot rocks on one side of the gap. Again Becca waited, but when he jumped down and climbed the rocks on the other side, she'd had enough and scrambled up after him. He was tracing his fingertip along one rock and nodding. To Becca the rock simply looked like a rock. Then Slade rubbed his finger over a dark splotch staining the gray stone.

"What's that?" she asked.

"Dried blood."

"I guess a small animal was caught here by a larger one."

"No," Slade said, rising.

"No? As in, that's not animal blood? It's human blood?"

He leaned back against the rocks and crossed his arms over his chest. "Frank's horse and, I imagine, your father's went down because of a trip wire."

Her eyes widened. "You're sure?"

"I am about Frank's horse. I'll check the place where your father was killed. The wire was secured on the other set of rocks, and laid on the ground across this gap. A man behind these rocks pulled the wire at just the right moment. In all the confusion no one saw him. No one saw the wire either, because he knew what he was doing. He raised it just enough to do the job. There are thin cuts across the front of Frank's horse's forelegs. They'll heal all right on their own."

Becca's knees weakened. "Dear God," she whispered, "then it's true. My father was murdered, and Frank was intentionally hurt."

"I'll make sure the clues are there concerning your father. Tell me where it happened and I'll come back out on my own. No sense putting yourself through that."

"I want to. I want to see the proof," she said vehemently. "Today. Right now."

"This isn't proof, Becca. It's cause. There's nothing here to link this to Folger."

"Of course it's Folger's work. He hired whoever did this."

"I'm sure he did."

"Well?"

"The man made one mistake. To pull the trip wire, you wrap it around the palm of your hand. A horse hitting that wire carries a lot of weight, and a smart man wears two pairs of heavy work gloves. This blood says that man didn't. Somewhere, there's a man with a deep cut across the palm of his hand."

"It's one of Folger's men, I know it is. Slade, the evidence of the trip wire is proof. It is, don't you see?"

"We can't ride onto Folger's land and demand to examine all of his men's hands."

"There must be *something* we can do."

"Tell our boys to keep their eyes open, whenever they're

in town, for someone with that kind of cut. Don't look so disappointed, Becca. It's a start. We know more than when we woke up this morning. But don't say anything about this to anyone we see today."

"Why not?"

"Because I said so. How far is it to the spot where your father was killed?"

"About a mile north."

"Are you sure you—"

"Yes, Slade, I want to see the proof that my father was murdered. I need to see it, understand?"

"All right. We'll—" His head snapped up, and he stared at a hill in the distance.

Becca looked too. "What is—Oh!"

In a blur of motion, Slade flung himself at her, hurling her to the ground and covering her body with his. Her hat rolled away as a shot rang out, ricocheting off the rocks where Slade had been standing.

"Don't move," he said.

Move? she thought in a rush of panic. She couldn't even breathe. The wind had been knocked out of her, and Slade was lying on top of her. His warm, tightly muscled body was pressed against hers. She could feel his heat, smell the aroma of sweat and leather and the unique scent that was pure male. She was staring at his throat, but then he tipped his head down to look at her, and she was gazing at his lips, so close to hers.

Their eyes met. Becca's heart beat wildly, and she wondered if it was from fear because someone had shot at them, or because she was lying beneath Slade Ironbow. He felt wonderful, heavy and male, rugged and taut . . .

Move, Ironbow! Slade yelled silently at himself. But Becca felt so good. She was shielded by the rocks. There was no excuse for him to keep her pinned to the ground, but she was gazing at him with those big green eyes. . . .

Slade didn't move. Becca didn't move. They continued

to stare at each other. Time lost meaning, and neither could have said if seconds or hours passed. Everything was still, quiet, and Becca was certain Slade would hear the rapid beating of her heart.

Nervously, she slid her tongue along her bottom lip.

Slade groaned, "Damn." Then lowered his head to claim her mouth with his.

Becca's eyes widened in shock, but in the next instant, her lashes drifted down. Her arms encircled Slade's neck, and he deepened the kiss. His tongue parted her lips with gentle insistence and delved into her mouth, and she complied willingly.

Shifting most of his weight to his forearms to keep from crushing her, Slade held her head in his hands. His tongue stroked hers in a rhythmic, seductive duel. The lips that had tortured him were now his. Heat gathered low in his body and his manhood swelled, straining against his pants and pressing into Becca's softness. He ached. He wanted. He burned with a need he'd never known before. All of her passion was desire now, not anger, and it was directed at him. She was responding totally to him in her innocence. Her innocence . . .

Slade fought against the haze of desire clouding his mind. He was losing control, and he never lost control. Not in anger, and sure as hell not in desire. Dammit, what was this woman doing to him!

He tore his mouth from hers, and in one jerky motion rolled off her and away. Drawing his knees up and draping his arms over them, he stared straight ahead, struggling to control his breathing, to control the aching want of his throbbing manhood.

Becca blinked, missing Slade's heat, his weight, the feel of his lips and tongue. Sitting up, she became aware of her trembling limbs, and aware of a curling, pulsing warmth deep within her. She looked at Slade from beneath her lashes. Tension seemed to emanate from him in waves.

"Slade?" she whispered, her voice quivering.

"That shouldn't have happened," he said harshly.

She frowned in confusion. "Why not?"

Slade snapped his head around to look at her. Desire still flushed her cheeks, her lips were swollen, and her eyes were smoky green with passion. His muscles tightened as he forced himself not to move, not to reach for her and claim those lips again. If he touched her now, he wouldn't stop until she was naked beneath him and he was burying his aching manhood deep inside her silken heat.

"Why not?" he repeated, with a sound of disgust. "Do you have any idea how close I came to taking you right here in the dirt?" He paused. "No, you don't know, do you? You're as innocent as a newborn babe. Hell."

"I certainly am not," she said indignantly. Oh, yes, she was, she admitted to herself. She'd been kissed a total of three times before today. Chaste little kisses pressed onto her lips by young men who'd taken her for an outing. Kisses that had left her disappointed. So, she *was* terribly innocent, but Slade Ironbow didn't have to be crude about it. "I'm a twenty-one-year-old woman, Mr. Ironbow," she said stiffly. "One does not live for twenty-one years without a certain amount of . . . experience in these matters."

"Now, is that a fact?" he asked dryly. "Well, good. Take off your clothes."

Her eyes widened. "What?"

He whirled and gripped her shoulders, hauling her up with him. "You felt me, didn't you?" he said, his voice ominously low. "You felt me hard against you, ready to have you. I want you. I ache with wanting you. Are you ready, Becca?" He reached for the top button of her shirt. "I'll do it for you, take off your clothes. Then I'll bury myself deep inside you and make love to you until the sun goes down. That will be fine with you, because you're so experienced in these matters."

"I . . . No, I've never . . . That is, I haven't . . ."

"Dammit," he roared, releasing her. "I know you haven't. I repeat—this should never have happened, and it won't happen again. I'm a man, not a boy. You'd best remember that. Don't kiss men the way you kissed me, Becca Colten, or you're going to get more than you bargained for. Now, stay here while I check for that gunman. In case you've forgotten, someone took a shot at us. Don't move one damn inch."

Becca opened her mouth, but before she could speak, Slade had disappeared around the rocks. She sighed and closed her mouth, realizing she wouldn't have known what to say anyway. She felt like a child, a naive, innocent child. She reached for her hat and plunked it on. Then again, she reasoned, she'd excited and aroused a man like Slade, so she must have kissed him as a woman would have. There was nothing childish about what she'd felt deep inside herself.

She tapped a fingertip against her chin. She should be ashamed of her behavior, she supposed, but she wasn't. Slade was obviously angry as blue blazes at her, but she wasn't angry at herself, nor sorry she'd kissed him. It had felt right, special, and if she could push back time and make the choice, she'd do it all again.

Because it was Slade.

It seemed to Becca that Slade had no sooner left than he returned, startling her out of her reverie.

"You weren't gone long," she said as he hunkered down beside her.

He glared at her. "I'd be breaking my own rules. I can't leave my . . . partner."

"Oh, that's right," she said sweetly. "And I'm your partner. Tsk, tsk, to think that you almost went off and left me all by my lonesome self."

"You're acting strange," he said, peering closely at her.

"Me? Don't be silly. You look like a brewing storm, so I decided someone has to be cheerful in this . . . partnership. Did you see anyone out there?"

"No. I made myself visible to give him another chance to shoot at me, but nothing happened. I figure he's long gone."

"You made yourself visible? So he could shoot at you? That doesn't sound very bright."

"My choices were limited," he said dryly. He pushed himself to his feet and extended his hand to her. "Let's go."

She placed her hand in his and allowed him to pull her to her feet. They were standing toe to toe, and she looked up at him, aware that he still held her hand.

"I'm not sorry, Slade," she said softly, "about what happened. You can holler your head off from here to Sunday, and I still won't be sorry."

He smiled. "I don't holler."

"You certainly do. You growl, too."

His dark eyebrows shot up. "Growl?" he repeated, releasing her hand.

"Yes. Growl."

His smile faded. "Becca, I was more angry at myself than at you. I should never have kissed you, because . . ." He took off his Stetson, raked his hand through his hair, then thrust his hat back on his head. "Let's go."

"Slade, wait." Placing her hand on his arm, she felt him flinch, his muscles tautening beneath her touch. "Can't we talk about this? Why do you feel you shouldn't have kissed me?"

"Dammit, Becca . . ."

"Why?" she asked, tightening her grip.

"I shouldn't have kissed you because I *wanted* to kiss you!" He jerked his arm free and started down the rocks. "Let's go. Now!"

Becca stared up at the sky. "He shouldn't have kissed me, because he *wanted* to kiss me," she repeated under her breath. "Therefore, he's angry because he kissed me. Heavens, what a complicated man."

"Becca!"

"I'm coming," she called, and scrambled down the rocks after Slade.

A short time later, Slade was once more carefully examining the shrub grass between two large sets of rocks. Becca had led him to the area where her father had been killed, and she stood quietly by the horses, watching.

It didn't take him long to find the evidence. He walked back to Becca, unable to keep his gaze from sliding over her, unable to keep from remembering how she had felt beneath him. Unable to forget how much he still wanted her.

"Slade?" she asked as he drew near. "What did you find?"

"Come on," he said gently, "let's get you out of here."

"No, tell me, please."

"It was a trip wire, Becca. Your father . . . was murdered."

She nodded, unable to speak as tears closed her throat. She mounted her horse and fiddled with the reins, not meeting Slade's gaze.

"Are you all right?" he asked quietly.

She nodded again. "Yes. I sensed it. I've never believed it was an accident. There's just something about actually hearing you say the words . . ." She paused to take a breath, then lifted her gaze to his. "I swear to heaven that Folger is going to pay for this. He's going to pay, Slade."

"He will, but you're going to have to be patient." He swung into his saddle. "We'll ride fence for a while now, see how the men are doing. Remember, don't say anything about us finding out about the trip wires."

"All right."

"Becca."

"Yes?"

"We'll get Folger."

"But what if we can't prove anything? What if—"

"We'll get him," Slade interrupted, a steely edge to his voice. "You have my word on that." He turned his horse and started away.

"Thank you, Slade Ironbow," Becca whispered, then nudged her horse to catch up with him.

Seven

In Dodge City, Kansas, people stood motionless on the wooden sidewalks, watching Doc Willis. He rode straight down the center of the dusty main street in a black buggy with a fancy top edged in fringe, a white horse pulling it.

When he halted in front of the Silver Spur, a collective gasp went up from the women. The men had a variety of reactions. Some nodded in approval, a few smiled enviously, and others shook their heads as they pictured Doc lying dead in the street after Slade Ironbow returned.

Doc jumped down from the buggy, tied the horse's reins to the hitching post, and strode forward to knock at the closed doors of the Spur.

Abe opened one of the doors. "Lord Almighty, you're back."

"I surely am," Doc said, smiling. "I've come calling on Miss Muldoon, Abe. I'd appreciate your letting me in, then informing her that I'm here."

Abe stuck his head out the door and glanced up and down the street. Then he looked at Doc again, grinning.

"I'll inform Miss Muldoon of your arrival, sir," Abe boomed, "and see if she will receive a gentleman this afternoon."

Someone on the street cackled with laughter.

Doc swept off his Stetson and stepped inside. "Gentleman?" he asked Abe.

Abe shrugged as he shut the door. "Lordy, you do have this town in a frenzy. Them chocolates—"

"Doc!"

Doc and Abe looked up to see Mattie hurrying down the stairs. She was wearing a pale green cotton day dress, and tortoiseshell combs held her auburn curls in an attractive, casual tumble on top of her head.

She was absolutely lovely, Doc thought. Whether she was wearing a simple frock or silk and feathers, she was the most beautiful woman in the world.

"Doc . . ." Mattie began, stopping in front of him.

"Jim," he said, smiling warmly at her. "Hello, Mattie. You're looking especially nice today. I've come calling to ask you to go on a picnic lunch with me."

Her eyes widened. "A picnic?"

"Yes, ma'am." He rocked back and forth on the balls of his feet, a very pleased expression on his face. "I have a fine lunch in a wicker basket out in the buggy. I'd be honored if you'd come with me."

"I've never been on a picnic," she said wistfully, then she blinked. "No, I can't. People will talk. They'll—"

"They'll be wishin' *they* was goin' on a picnic," Abe said. "Surely is a fine day for it."

"It is, indeed," Doc said.

"Well, I do need to talk to you . . ." Mattie shook her head. "No, absolutely not. Since you're obviously not using the two cents worth of brains God gave you, Jim Willis, then I'll have to do it for you. You're making the biggest mistake of your life, and I won't be a party to it. I will *not* walk through that door with you, and have the whole town see us leaving together to go on a picnic."

"You're a strong, stubborn woman, Mattie," Doc said. "I know when I'm beat. Abe, if you'll be so kind as to go out to the buggy and get the picnic basket, Mattie and I will have our lunch right here inside the Spur."

"Sure thing," Abe said, starting toward the door.

"No!" Mattie yelled. "Abraham, don't you move another inch." Abe stopped and looked at her, his eyebrows raised questioningly. "Doc . . . Jim, you can't stay in here while the Spur is closed. People will assume that we're . . . I want you to leave right this minute."

"Now, Mattie," Doc said, "as much as I'd like to grant your every wish, it's only fitting that I have a say in our relationship, too. You said you wouldn't go on a picnic with me, so the picnic is coming in here. Seems to me that is a fair give-and-take bargain. It is also my final word on the subject."

"You're crazy," she exclaimed. "You can't stay in here now."

"Then I suggest we proceed with the original plan, and have our picnic outside in the sunshine." He crooked his arm. "Miss Muldoon? Shall we go? We'll talk during lunch. You did say you needed to speak to me, didn't you?" He lifted her hand and placed it on his arm. "Abraham, take charge of the Spur."

"Oh, yes, sir," Abe said, chuckling. "Don't be givin' this place another thought. Enjoy your picnic."

"We certainly will," Doc said.

"But . . ." Mattie began, then shook her head and closed her mouth. Outside, she glanced down the street. "Oh, Jim," she whispered, "everyone is staring. I knew it. I just knew it would be like this."

"Hold your head up high, Mattie Muldoon," he said sternly. "Are you going to let some nosy gossips spoil the first picnic you've ever been on?"

She looked at him for a long moment, then lifted her chin. "No, I'm not." Her eyes sparkled as she saw the buggy and white horse. "Oh, what a fine buggy. I've never ridden in anything so nice-looking."

Doc assisted her onto the seat, then joined her. Once again he rode straight down the middle of the street. Mattie kept her head high, training her eyes on one of the horse's ears. They were at last out of Dodge and away from the buzzing crowd, and she sank back against the seat with a sigh.

"Doc . . . Jim . . . I'm going to say this again. You're making a terrible mistake. I had to speak to you about this. Maybe it's not too late. Maybe. If you stop this foolishness right now, the town folks might forget in time, and your reputation won't be ruined."

Doc turned the horse onto a narrow dirt road and kept going.

"Are you listening to me, Jim?"

"Look at those spring wildflowers," he said. "Fields of them in every color of the rainbow. Now, that is a pretty sight."

"James Willis, you're *not* listening to me!"

"No."

"You sound like Slade," she said, unable to contain a bubble of laughter. " 'Yep' and 'No' are his two favorite words."

"Yep," Doc said, and grinned at her.

Her smile faded, and she sighed. "Oh, Jim, how can I make you understand that this is wrong, and hopeless?"

"You can't. I love you, Mattie."

He reined in the horse beneath a large tree and jumped down from the seat. After securing the reins to a branch, he came around to her side and extended his arms to her.

She placed her hands on his shoulders as he gripped her waist and lifted her off the seat to the ground. He didn't release her, nor did Mattie drop her hands from his shoulders.

They stood there in the shade of the tree, surrounded by wildflowers that filled the air with a delicate fragrance. Bees hummed, birds chirped and sang, a sassy squirrel chattered.

Jim dipped his head and covered Mattie's lips with his.

All thoughts and fears fled Mattie's mind as her lashes drifted down. She was instantly swept away to the rosy place that only Jim could take her to. She returned his kiss with all of her love, feeling safe and protected in the circle of his arms.

He slowly lifted his head. "Let's . . ." He cleared his throat. "Let's get our picnic lunch." He drew his thumb lightly over her lips before reaching for a blanket and the wicker basket that were tucked behind the seat. "There's a nice group of trees over there."

Mattie nodded, unable to speak. Her knees were trembling from the passionate kiss, her heart was racing. She walked through the flowers at Jim's side in silence.

They ate in silence, too, their picnic of fried chicken, biscuits, and fresh fruit. At last Doc pushed his food away and took Mattie's hand.

"Do you believe that I love you?" he asked.

"Yes," she said softly.

"Do you . . . care for me at all? I mean, do you feel *something* for me? Please, tell me the truth. You kiss me as though you do, but I need to hear the words."

She looked away, her eyes misting with tears.

"Mattie?"

"Whatever I may or may not feel for you isn't important."

"Yes, it is! If you love me, then together we can do anything. Nothing can stop us from finding our happiness. Oh, Mattie, please, say the words, tell me that what I see in your eyes, feel in your kiss is true."

"No," she said, shaking her head. "No, I . . . don't . . ." The tears spilled onto her cheeks. ". . . don't love you, Jim."